BUILD
UNIVERS

Colin Ridyard

The Flumpkin and Clutterbutt

Appreciation Society

Enjoy the book!
Best wishes
Colin Ridyard

europe books

© 2021 **Europe Books**| London

www.europebooks.co.uk | info@europebooks.co.uk

ISBN 979-12-201-1129-4

First edition: September 2021

Distribution for the United Kingdom: **Vine House Distribution ltd**

Printed for Italy by *Rotomail Italia S.p.A. - Vignate (MI)*

Stampato presso *Rotomail Italia S.p.A. - Vignate (MI)*

The Flumpkin and Clutterbutt

Appreciation Society

CHAPTER ONE - The Inquisition

"Guy Foulkstone, isn't it? Take a seat. Miss Creeveley will see you when she has spoken to the others. I wouldn't get too comfortable if I were you!"

Cackling like a witch, Miss Macbeth, the Headmistress's secretary, barely looked up as she hammered away at her keyboard, and while the corridor at Eleven Hills High was warm with the smell of pizza, I felt a wintry chill run down my spine. Here I was, in deeper doo-doo than the day Dewie Deuterium, the demented dodo physicist, decided to develop a dodo-killing death ray. Diana Belmont had already gone home in floods of tears. Poor kid! As if she didn't have enough problems!

I checked my mobile. The network was still down. Two days now! How could I call my Mum and tell her about all this trouble with Creeveley over a book... a kids' book at that?

I suppose this business really started four years ago when Melvyn Mystico came and visited us at our then primary school. By 'us', I mean myself, Diana, Will Thompkins and Emma Nightingale. We'd always been friends and used to hang out together at each other's houses or in the local youth club.

A children's story writer, Mr Mystico asked us at the time what we thought would make a great novel for children. As kids, it was a totally brilliant experience! We came up with all sorts of ideas for names and plots and he listened intently and took notes and we drew pictures and comic strips. Well, I sort of drew pictures anyway. The sum total of my artistic ability would fit on the back of a Lilliputian postage stamp! Anyway, six months later, as reward for our efforts, we each received a signed copy of *Flumpkin and Clutterbutt Get into Trouble* through the letter-box. Elated by our contributions, we formed the Flumpkin and Clutterbutt Appreciation Society.

"Wipe that stupid smile off your face, idiot boy!" hissed the secretary, her eyes still firmly on her computer screen. Not even thinking I stuck my tongue out at her! Just like Flumpkin and Clutterbutt!

Just so you know, Flumpkin and Clutterbutt are two mischievous boy fairies. Clutterbutt was Diana's idea and Flumpkin was mine. I'd originally called him 'Stinkerbell' but Mr Mystico insisted we re-christen him 'for commercial reasons' and so Emma came up with the name 'Flumpkin' after her pet gerbil. One other thing we need to get straight - forget everything else you have read before; fairies do not have wings!

Anyway, I could still remember the first chapter in the book and I gave a low chuckle. The ice-cold glance from Miss Creeveley's secretary made me quickly put my hand to my mouth though.

The first chapter went something like this:

"Begone, and never darken North Fairyland again with your horrid antics!"

Constable Woodencop frogmarched the two fairies right up to the silver gate.

Flumpkin in his frilly snowdrop shirt groaned.

Clutterbutt in his red poppy-petal jacket gulped.

Expulsion into the world outside seemed a pretty harsh penalty. All they'd done was magic an unmovable beard onto a portrait of Queen Mabiley the Third. It wasn't really their fault the wand-fight had perhaps gotten a little too out of hand.

"Oh come on, please," moaned Flumpkin, his blue eyes wet with tears. "How were we to know the anti-magic charm had been lifted for restoration..."

"... and no one told us the urn was a four-hundred-year-old antique," added Clutterbutt, wiping his wet cheeks with a pudgy hand.

"That urn..." spluttered Constable Woodencop. "That urn just happened to be part of Princess Lavendar's priceless Mercutio collection. If you ask me; what you did in that royal flowerpot should be punishable by... by... sixty years in the Crungeon Dungeon."

He exhaled deeply, then added, "As for that flatulence charm on the whoopee-cushion – the Lord Lieutenant is still undergoing intensive therapy. Believe me, at the moment, you are both far safer outside of Fairyland than inside and to prevent your return we're sealing the gate..."

The school bell rang for dinner, and I heard the muffled clatter of chairs and desks and laughter. We weren't in primary school anymore and somehow Year Ten in Eleven Hills High made fairy stories and the Appreciation Society seem so yesterday and distant. I was in the school rugby team now, and this sort of thing wasn't exactly discussed in a boys' changing room after a match - or ever for that matter!

Had things followed a normal progression, my friends and I would probably have grown out of Mr Mystico's novels completely and all this trouble wouldn't have happened. However, a month or two ago, we'd been given an English assignment and had to write a summary on a book of our choice. Will and Emma suggested a Flumpkin and Clutterbutt story and I agreed. Not so much because I still liked the fairy pair. More because it seemed such an easy choice given our past association with Mr Mystico.

I remember in the library, I was busily glancing at some of the boys' rugby magazines in the foyer when I heard Will gasp. For a moment, I thought he needed his asthma pump.

"L-Look at the shelves, Guy," he stammered, wiping his glasses and putting them back on again. "L-Look how empty they are!"

My heart nearly leapt into my mouth. Huge gaping gaps stood between the few books left. And titles like *My Parents Work Hard in the Factory* and *Robin and Ryan Volunteer to Clean the Park* were the only ones that glared out at us.

"Well, I suppose a lot of people are doing the assignment," I suggested.

"I don't think so," said Will, regaining his composure. "Look over there."

I turned my head and saw literally hundreds of books stacked high on a trolley. Surrounding it were bulging black bin bags; some with book corners sticking through holes punctured in the thin stretched plastic.

"Good, isn't it? Fawksey," said a sneering voice behind me.

I recognised the voice immediately, and my skin crawled. It belonged to our classmate, Terry Smythers-McCoy; and here, I use the word 'mate' in its loosest possible sense. He stood there, grinning all over his freckled-face – the sort of grin that had 'hit me' written all over it.

"About time we got rid of all this old-fashioned rubbish, don't you think?" he went on, with his nose in the air. "I mean stories about wizards, aliens, fairies – what inappropriate nonsense!"

Will chortled.

"I'd rather read *Timon of Athens* in binary code than Robin and Ryan, given the choice," he said.

Smythers-McCoy's eyes narrowed.

"Robin and Ryan are two upstanding truly inspirational teenagers who teach children all that is right in a modern Democracy," he said in a snooty voice. "They are thoroughly decent and always do what is right..."

Will and I didn't bother to stay around and hear him finish. Instead, we approached the librarians' desk.

"What's happening?" I asked, waving my hand in the direction of the trolley.

"Can't you read?" said a stern-looking librarian pointing to a sign on the wall. It read:

By order of the Supreme City Council, all Public Libraries are instructed henceforth that they may only put on display those books permitted by The Council. A comprehensive list of all approved texts is to be found on the website at www.entertainmentministry.gov.uk.

"Does that mean they're being thrown out?" I asked her.

"Actually, no," she replied. "They are going on permanent loan to Lord Mashley, second in line to the throne of Spudley in the land of the Potato People – of course they're getting thrown out, you silly boy!"

"Could we possibly take some of them?" whispered Will.

"Go on then," said the librarian in a low voice. "But don't tell anyone!"

We grabbed a handful of our once-favourite Mr Mystico books and scarpered. My haul included one we hadn't actually read before about a cheeky squirrel who painted on old buildings with his tail and ended up putting on an exhibition at the National Art Gallery.

To my surprise, I enjoyed reading about Splooshy the squirrel so much I shared it with Will and the girls. The original idea of Flumpkin and Clutterbutt was quickly forgotten, and we finished a joint assignment on Splooshy's artistic antics last week with no more trouble than a little paper cut on my middle finger.

Unfortunately, Mr Robson, the English teacher, liked Diana's report so much, he asked her to read it out in class yesterday. And that's where the trouble really began because somebody went and reported 'inappropriate book use' to the headmistress (I could guess who).

So there I was, waiting for the Headmistress to call me in. I still couldn't believe it. Since when was doing an English assignment on a story book an expellable offence?

The door to the headmistress' office flew open and out stormed Will and Emma. Both pale as ghosts.

"Suspended! Watch out!" mouthed Emma, her bright green eyes flashing.

"Silence!" hissed the secretary from behind the reception desk.

I watched my two friends disappear down the corridor and then turn right through the glass-panelled entrance. My heart sank. They'd just been suspended for reading a book! And then another chill ran down my spine.

"How long for," I wondered. "And why was I being seen separately?"

Was I going to be expelled?

An image of the crooked turrets of Saint Tremerwick's came to mind, and I shuddered. No way could I ever go back there!

The wait to be called in seemed like a whole hour, but in reality, it must have been only five minutes. At last, the secretary's phone rang, and she looked up at me and said, "Mrs Creeveley will see you now."

With a low groan, I got up off the chair and looked towards the entrance where my friends had disappeared. Perhaps I could make a run for it or feign some emergency or something.

"No point in waiting around," said the secretary with another nasty cackle. "You'll only make her angrier."

Just as I turned to go, something at the entrance caught my eye. Two tall figures had suddenly appeared and were waving at me in the distance. One wore a red poppy-coloured jacket and the other had on what looked like a white baggy frilly shirt.

Who on earth were they?

I blinked, and the next instant, the pair of them started dancing something like a cross between the can-can and a mutated Macaroon stomp. Perhaps the school was putting on a concert? It had been at least two years since they'd done one.

"GUY FOULKSTONE!" came a sudden shrill voice from the direction of Mrs Creeveley's office. "I WON'T ASK AGAIN; WILL YOU COME IN HERE AT ONCE!"

"C-coming," I stammered.

CHAPTER TWO – In the Dragon's Den

"Sit down, boy!"

Mrs Creevely stood behind a dark leather-topped bow-legged table and pointed at a low seated chair. Had it been any lower, in fact, my knees would have touched my chest.

She looked down at me through thick horn-rimmed glasses; though they weren't as thick as the blueberry lipstick she wore, which in turn wasn't as revolting as the plum chequered dress suit or the bleach blond beehive hairdo that screamed, "fashion disaster" to each and every portrait in the office. Small wonder all the old headmasters and headmistresses in the pictures seemed to be averting their eyes!

"Well, isn't this cosy?" said Mrs Creevely at last. "You and me, here alone to talk about life, the universe and what makes the world go round."

"P-pardon?" I said.

"Isn't it amazing," she went on, "how you can have the best soil, the best gardeners and the best seeds in the world – yet for all that labour, your prize begonias and roses are stifled by the weeds in their midst – do you know what one needs to do to weeds, Mr Foulkstone?"

"Pick them out," I suggested.

"Precisely, only not just pick them, Mr Foulkstone – oh no, they have to be pulled up by their roots and thrown on the compost then shredded and diced and mulched so they cannot contaminate your prize flowers anymore.

"And that is exactly the philosophy I have here at Eleven Hills High; weed out the troublemakers and give the best pupils the chance to bloom into prize citizens who will do their city and their country proud. That, you see, is how the true modern Democracy thrives in the chaos of today."

Like a psycho spider contemplating a fly caught in a web, Mrs Creevely fell silent and put her hands together at the fingertips, watching me through her big black eyes. I had the feeling she was waiting for me to say something, but I honestly couldn't think of anything. Who cared about politics, anyway?

Why couldn't people be like Flumpkin and Clutterbutt? They had no qualms about life's ups and downs. For example, there was the time they were getting insulted in Ye Olde Gaye Wood:

The rabbits all joined in with the chorus of "who ate all the carrots?" and Flumpkin could see Clutterbutt getting redder and redder to the point where steam was actually coming out of his pointy ears.

"Don't let them get to you," he whispered as about a dozen squirrels joined paws with the rabbits and began dancing around them. "They're only woodland creatures after all."

"Hey, Clutterbutt," spluttered Rodney Bobtail over his shoulder. "Since you're too fat to fly, maybe you should go over to Dover. They've got big ships there that'll be able to 'fairy' you around – geddit, lads?"

"That does it! Shalakazam!"

Before Flumpkin could stop him, Clutterbutt flicked his wand and sent a trail of multi-coloured stars at the bothersome bunny. Rodney Bobtail let out a squeal and started bounding around, holding his singed tail. A faint trail of wispy smoke followed in his wake.

Suddenly, there was an almighty crash and two large hooded figures in livery green appeared in the forest. Each had a bow and arrow levelled at the two fairies.

"Oh no, not more wood elves," wailed Flumpkin.

"How dare you use magic on those poor innocent woodland creatures," snarled the first figure.

"Let's scarper," said Clutterbutt...

"Really, this is nothing to smile about, Mr Foulkstone," snapped Mrs Creevely, in a tone that yanked me out of my daydream. "I've already suspended three of your classmates and you are this far from joining them."

She held her forefinger tip bare millimetres away from her thumb then added, "I think the time has come for you to decide what sort of a plant you want to be here at Eleven Hills High – tell me, Guy, what is it your parents do?"

"My father's a businessman," I replied, feeling an angry flush of my cheeks.

"And what sort of business is he in?"

"Precious stones, rocks, rare minerals, that sort of thing."

"And your mother?"

"I don't see her much; she flies helicopters in the army."

Something twinged inside my stomach as I gave her the answer. It had been at least three months since I'd written to my mother and, whilst I'd spoken to her on the phone a few weeks ago, the mobile network was now down.

"So tell me, there's your mother fighting for freedom and democracy in a far off country – how do you think she would feel if she were to learn her only son had been suspended from school for vandalism and wanton destruction of private property?"

For a second, the accusation barely registered.

"P-pardon?" I spluttered. The news hit me like a ton of tumbling tarantulas.

Mrs Creevely threw down some photographs and they hit the table top with a loud "whap!" I examined them briefly. They didn't amount to much. Just a couple of old buildings daubed in graffiti. However, on closer examination, I realised one very official-looking building had a picture of a silver bowl filled with acorns painted on it. Another, a police station of all places, had a very lifelike picture of a chestnut tree. A third, the mobile mast on Warren Hill reduced to a charred wreckage and some half-eaten roasted chestnuts. Suddenly it all fitted into place; the homework, the assignment on Splooshy the Squirrel, the lack of phone reception.

"Hang on a minute," I said, my voice still a little quaky. "Do you really think me and my friends did this?"

"Who else could have done it but you and that stupid Mr Mystico Appreciation Society?"

"Anyone could've," I replied. "And anyway, the *Clutterbutt and Flumpkin* Appreciation Society doesn't meet anymore." I deliberately emphasised Clutterbutt and Flumpkin.

"And tell me, Mr Foulkstone, where would the perpetrators have gotten the idea?"

"Well, there's this bit in Splooshy the Squirrel..." I began remembering how he'd painted pistachios and acorns on the town hall.

"Precisely," snapped Mrs Creeveley, with a hint of triumph in her voice. "And do you know how many copies of Splooshy the Squirrel there are, here in Manchester?"

I shook my head.

"Obviously, the author is a complete waste of space because there's just the two of them. One in the city library and one in Warren Hill town library; both of which were scheduled for shredding – but clearly, one of them seems to have found its way into the hands of you and your friends and like all nonsense about wizards, aliens, magic and talking animals, it has led you down the road of wantonness and destruction.

"Now, Mr Foulkstone, do you know why I have decided not to suspend you?"

I shook my head.

Mrs Creeveley opened her mouth as though about to speak when suddenly there was an almighty clattering sound from outside coupled with what seemed like a herd of cows mooing. Ten seconds later, the door burst open and the secretary half staggered and half fell through the entrance.

"Mrs Creeveley," she shrieked. "Come quick, someone's just let loose a herd of wildebeest in the school!"

The Headmistress's jaw dropped wide open.

"You," she snapped, turning to me.

"Don't look at me," I retorted. "Where would I find a herd of wildebeest?"

"Get back to your class immediately, Guy," she snapped. And then, without another word, she disappeared through the door, closely followed by her near-hysterical secretary.

A minute later, I got up and left the room, too. Out in the corridor, I could hear the clanging of metal, and the tinkling of crockery from the direction of the canteen. Teachers and children were running in all directions, some wearing half-eaten pizza, baked beans and mashed potatoes. I wondered how near Mrs Creeveley was to bringing the rampant herd of wildebeest under control. More to the point, how on earth did they get into the school in the first place? The nearest zoo was miles away.

Something told me there wouldn't be much to be gained in staying for lessons that afternoon; and anyway, my friends had all gone home. For the first time in my life, within school time and with absolutely no regrets whatsoever, I headed for the gates. Emma lived nearest to the school and I had a thousand questions going round in my mind.

19

CHAPTER THREE – Lunch with Emma

It was only five minutes later that, whilst walking along the pavement by the main road, I realised my crime. I knew playing truant was wrong; but there was a good reason. And as if to emphasise the point, two police motorcycles raced past, sirens wailing and heading in the direction I'd just come from. They didn't give me a second glance which I suppose made things sort of alright. Their uniforms were a little curious. I'd never seen British policemen in leather jackets and leather trousers before. They looked not too dissimilar in fact to one of those 1970s disco pop groups my dad was so fond of. How embarrassing!

Two minutes later, I turned right into Cedar Grove and walked up the short drive to Number Fourteen. The lawn was neatly mowed and the precision-cut borders were full of roses and lots of other flowers that I didn't recognise.

From past visits, I knew Emma's house wasn't that big; it only had five bedrooms. Nevertheless, it was fairly modern and was always spotlessly clean inside.

I didn't need to knock. There was a thunder of feet on the stairs and the front door burst open. Before I could say anything, Emma had me in a massive hug and just about squeezed every last breath out of my lungs.

"Did the old hag suspend you, too," she asked, letting me go at last.

I shook my head.

"She suspended me and Will for a week each," said Emma. "But get this, she's gone and suspended Diana for a fortnight! Her dad's gonna flip! Oh, Guy, I can't even begin to believe Diana's been spray-painting graffiti on walls; it's just not her style – her dad won't even let her out of the house after nine."

"I don't believe she'd do it either," I said. "I'm just sorry I took that book."

"Do you think somebody else read Splooshy the Squirrel and got the idea?"

"I don't know," I replied. "There can't have been that many people who read it, especially as there were so few copies about."

"Do you think Terry Smythers-McCoy might have done the graffiti so he could get her into trouble?"

I thought for a minute, but it just didn't make any sense. My earlier assumption that he'd reported us for reading a censored book hadn't been wholly correct and now, come to think of it, Diana hadn't mentioned the fact that Splooshy painted acorns in silver bowls during her class talk. Something else occurred to me. The Splooshy the Squirrel book hadn't been taken out of the library before because there were no date stamps on the inside cover slip.

"No, there's no way Terry'd have known," I said. "And anyway," I added after giving my explanation. "Terry's just like me in that respect, we both have the artistic ability of a whale with its flippers in plaster."

Emma giggled.

"Probably why creepy Creevely didn't suspend you as well then, she must have known you couldn't have done it.

"Fancy something to eat?"

Emma must have heard my stomach rumbling because I was absolutely starving, and whilst she cooked some sausages and bacon, I told her all about the herd of wildebeest in the school.

"Sounds like the sort of thing you'd read in a Flumpkin and Clutterbutt story," she laughed, emptying some tinned tomatoes into a pyrex dish and putting them in the microwave. "With a bit of luck, they'll close the school for a week and I won't miss any lessons."

The mention of the two fairies reminded me of the two people dancing the mutated Macaroon back at school, and I told Emma about them.

"I agree," she said once I'd finished. "They were probably practising for a concert or something – do you remember that version of My Fair Lady the sixth form did just before creepy Creevely arrived?"

The microwave pinged. Emma plated up the food then added, "Come on, let's eat this before it goes cold."

We ate lunch in Emma's large dining room. Her parents both worked late in an electrical store, and her twin brothers were away at university, so it was just the two of us. Emma was a smashing cook and the sausages literally melted in my mouth. Then, when I thought I couldn't eat anymore, she produced two large wedges of Black Forest gateau with 'eat me' written all over them.

I was just licking the last few crumbs off my fingers when we heard a knock at the door. Emma went into the hall to answer it then let out an exclamation.

"Oh cripes, it's the fuzz!"

My heart nearly leapt into my mouth. Emma had good reason to be away from school, but I didn't. Fortunately, my school bag stood in the corner, and I immediately hit upon the idea of saying I'd brought some work over for her.

A few seconds later, two policemen wearing leathers came into the dining room. I'm sure they were the same ones I'd seen earlier. They looked around the place, nodded approvingly at the décor, then sat down at the table. The first one removed his sunglasses to reveal a pair of the deepest grey eyes imaginable.

"Good afternoon," he said. "Allow me to introduce myself, I am Constable Lightfoot. Would I be right to say I am addressing Mr Guy Foulkstone and Miss Emma Nightingale?"

I nodded and, at the same time, felt myself go cold. There was something about his tone I didn't like.

"…The same Guy Foulkstone and Emma Nightingale who formed the Clutterbutt and Flumpkin Appreciation Society?"

Emma gulped. This had to have had something to do with the graffiti. True, we had formed the appreciation society back in primary school in a vain attempt to get more people to buy Mr Mystico's books but we didn't go around vandalising police stations. I guess we sort of felt a kind of loyalty towards Mr Mystico back then, but now, well, it wasn't the sort of thing you really admitted to!

"We had nothing to do with it," I blurted out. "The graffiti, I mean."

The policeman laughed.

"My dear boy," he said airily. "We don't for one minute suspect you personally of having painted that graffiti, oh no, no, no, no, no!" He laughed again.

"That's right," added the second policeman with a dismissive flick of his wrist. "Your headmistress invited us in earlier and showed us some of your artwork from the last few weeks. I must say, your version of The Sunflowers had some very – er – unique qualities?"

The fist policeman put his hand over his mouth and coughed. His pale cheeks went red and I had the distinct impression he was trying not to laugh.

"Why are you here then?" asked Emma, looking them up and down suspiciously.

"We're here to warn you about two dangerous escaped lunatics."

"Very dangerous escaped lunatics," added the second policeman. "We've been after them on and off for a few years now."

"You think these people are behind the graffiti?" I asked.

"Without a doubt – one looks about sixteen or seventeen; has a very baggy frilly white shirt; blue eyes and a thick mop of black hair with the odd plat sticking out."

Emma and I both looked at each other, obviously thinking the same thing.

"Yes," said the second policeman in an airy exasperated tone. "He dresses and acts just like Flumpkin the Fairy and has a very unhealthy obsession with Melvyn Mystico novels, just like his partner in crime, too, in fact."

"Who," added the first policeman. "Has a large build; looks about the same age; wears a bright red jacket; has green eyes; is constantly changing his hairstyle and has delusions that he's Clutterbutt."

"They're not just wanted for vandalism," said the first policeman. "They're also wanted for animal cruelty and countless other crimes, too."

"The herd of wildebeest?" I ventured.

Both men nodded.

"So you see," went on the first policeman. "We want you to be on your guard just in case they approach you. And if they do, we want you to contact us on this number."

"Why would they approach us?" asked Emma as they handed us each a card.

"Duh," said the second policeman. "'Clutterbutt and Flumpkin Go To America', in the credits where Mystico names you both and thanks to you for forming the Flumpkin and Clutterbutt Appreciation Society.

"We're just worried that in their delusional state, they might try and contact you and if they do, it might be dangerous for you."

I was just about to tell them about the two people I saw in school dancing the Macaroon stomp when I caught sight of Emma shushing her finger to her lip.

"Well then," she said in a grown-up voice. "I'm sure you two marvellous officers have a lot more investigations to make, and I can assure you if we see sight or sound of the two dreadful people you mentioned, we will contact you directly."

She looked at the card and added, "Constable Lightfoot, is there anything else we can do for you?"

"You could tell me where your parents bought that superb crystal vase," said Constable Lightfoot, getting up to leave and pointing towards some flowers on the windowsill. "And I must say, I simply adore the plum and gold frond wallpaper in this room."

"There is one other thing," said the second policeman. "Your friend, Diana Belmont; she lives in Concrete Close – could you warn her, too? We'd go ourselves only they won't let us in without a dozen riot vans as backup."

I remained at the table whilst the two officers were shown out. However, when Emma returned, she had a very puzzled expression on her face.

"If they were real policemen," she declared. "Then I'm Queen Mabiley the Third, complete with beard."

"They looked real to me," I said.

"The trouble with you boys is you have absolutely no sense of fashion and style. Since when do policemen wear poulaines?"

"What are poulaines?" I asked.

"Pointy shoes like they wore in Medieval times – when did you last see a policeman wearing pointy shoes, navy blue suede ones at that?"

Things were starting to get even more puzzling: first the graffiti; then the rampant wildebeest, and now people pretending to be policemen and looking for escaped lunatics who were pretending to be fairy tale characters. I tell you, my day couldn't have gotten any sillier.

"Come on," said Emma. "I really think we need to go over and see Diana and warn her about those two lunatics like those two weird coppers asked. Will was heading that way too when he left me, so he's probably still there."

"Couldn't we phone her?" I asked, wondering if I could also get a message to my mum in the meantime.

"No, landlines are down, too," Emma replied.

A trip to the council houses in Concrete Close didn't really appeal to me but the thought of Emma walking alone there appealed to me even less. And anyway, Diana was our friend and right now, probably needed us more than ever - especially if her dad had found out she'd been suspended.

CHAPTER FOUR – A Visit to Concrete Close

An uncommonly thick mist descended as we turned down the badly-cracked pavement leading into Concrete Close. Despite it being mid-afternoon in the middle of June, it was uncharacteristically dark; the few unvandalised street lights left were on and casting eerie shadows in their wake. The tall council houses loomed like shadowy monoliths in all directions and one could easily have gotten lost.

On the opposite side of the road, half a dozen tall shadowy figures in hoodies had congregated under one street light. One of them pointed in our direction as we walked past, and as one, they moved slowly toward us, menacingly, like a pride of hungry lions stalking a zebra.

"Guy," whispered Emma.

"I know," I replied. "Keep walking."

Abruptly, we opened the battered gate to Number Thirty-Two and our pursuers stopped dead in their tracks. It was this fact and the derelict Ford Capri on bricks that told us we were at Diana's house because none of the properties in Concrete Close had numbers on their gates or walls. Some said it was due to vandalism, others said it was just to confuse the police and the debt collectors. I didn't know myself whether this was true or not; however, I always felt a cold feeling of emptiness about the place.

Emma knocked softly on the blue front door and we both cringed at the echo. Soft footsteps pattered in the hallway beyond, and the door opened to reveal a small face with tousled black hair and big black eyes. A smell of stale beer and cigarette smoke filled the air.

"Hi Joey," whispered Emma. "Is your sister in?"

"Yes, she's in the back shed with Will, be quiet when you walk through though, 'cos Dad's asleep."

I remembered the last time Diana's dad had been woken up and shivered.

We used to hold regular Clutterbutt and Flumpkin Appreciation Society meetings in Diana's back shed and one day, we'd read *Clutterbutt and Flumpkin Cause an International Incident* together. I remembered how as we left through Diana's front room, Will and I began laughing about a leg charm they'd put on the famous Mona Lisa painting. I could still remember how it had been chased all around Paris by the French policemen and museum officials. A shudder ran down my spine when I recalled how the next minute, we heard this tremendous roar like a bull and saw Diana's dad exploding out of the leather sofa brandishing an empty beer bottle.

Will and I had never run so fast in our lives. He only chased us out of the house and through the garden gate, but that was scary enough. When we summoned up the courage to go back to apologise three months later, he just patted us on the backs, made us a cup of tea and told us not to be so silly.

Emma and I tiptoed past Diana's snoring father, taking care not to kick any of the empty beer bottles in the process. A battered TV in the corner was still on and quietly reporting how thousands of people were undemocratically congregating on Stonehenge for the Summer Solstice in a few days and how the police were bravely stopping them from doing so with truncheons, tasers, tear gas and water cannons.

Quiet as mice in a kitchen cat cookery conference, we tiptoed through the back door then stopped abruptly. There in the dim light stood Diana's back shed. It emitted an eldritch green glow through the curtained windows that shimmered in the afternoon mist like a halo.

"God, that's spooky," whispered Emma.

"Isn't it," I agreed. Then added, "Why not do the old appreciation society knock for fun?"

"Go on, then."

I put my left palm on the door; then tapped the back of the hand with my right palm; next, I rotated my left palm back and forth to give another tap-tap followed by several more left and right palm taps in quick succession.

We heard some shuffling and some voices from inside, then after what seemed an age, the door opened. Diana stood in the dim eldritch light; her short black hair and black eyes shining like polished obsidian. Two steps behind her stood Will, polishing his glasses. Short and stocky with strawberry blond hair pulled back in a pony-tail, he had a strange look about his eyes I hadn't seen before.

"I'm so glad you both came," whispered Diana. "You're not going to believe what's happened!"

"Ta-raa!" said Will pointing his open hand to a battered sofa.

From behind the battered sofa emerged two familiar yet also very unfamiliar teenagers. The red jacket on one and the white shirt on the other were a dead giveaway.

"The escaped lunatics!" I gasped, taking a backward step.

"Pardon?" said Will.

"It's Flumpkin and Clutterbutt!" assured Diana.

"Don't be so silly," chided Emma. "Fairies don't exist in real life."

The second she finished her sentence, the teenager who looked like Flumpkin somersaulted over the sofa and dropped to the floor like a street dancing sack of spuds. "I'm dying! I'm dying!" He squealed, writhing around like a turbo-charged cheetah on an ice-skating rink.

"You fool," said the chubby teenager, running his hands through what looked like fluorescent-green hair. "Do you realise every time you say you don't believe in fairies, a fairy actually dies!"

"I'm s-sorry," whispered Emma.

At that, the Flumpkin teenager did a handstand, span on his head and jumped up with the agility of a break dancing squirrel. He gave his friend a high five and said, "Bad fairy!"

"Badder fairy!" said the Clutterbutt teenager with a mischievous grin.

"Look," I said, keeping my voice down low. "You honestly don't expect us to believe you're both fairies…"

"Honest, Guy," whispered Will. "They're the real deal."

My nose wrinkled.

"OK," retorted Emma facing the two intruders with her chin in the air. "If you're both fairies; why don't you show us some magic."

"Easy," said Flumpkin, reaching towards the side of her face. "Abracadabra and incantations old, make this disbeliever give me gold."

He flicked his wrist and pulled a gold coin from behind her ear with a resounding "pop", then passed it on to me. One side had the words, "Queen Mabiley the Second, Defender of Magyck Most Benevolent" surrounding a young-looking queen's head. The other side had a picture of a lion and indicated a value of fifty guineas in old-fashioned writing. I was momentarily reminded of my grandfather, who used to do the same trick.

"Come on," I said with a grin. "That's not real magic. Even I can do that."

Bluetacked on the far wall was a badly-put-together cardboard doll of Clutterbutt. I'd made it back in primary school on the day Mr Mystico had visited us. The index finger on my left hand twinged a bit, and I distinctly remembered accidentally cutting myself with the craft knife when cutting the cardboard and spilling a few drops of crimson on Mr Mystico's notes.

"Tell you what," I said, pointing at the far wall. "Make that doll run around the shed like you did with the Mona Lisa in "International Incident" and then I just might believe you."

Flumpkin's shoulders slumped.

"Slight problem," he said. "That's a Level Three spell. Anything over Level Two and the Gaye Wood elves would be here in a flash; they've been following us around for the last three years."

"Yes," added Clutterbutt. "And if they catch us, they'll lock us in the keys and throw away the jail and all we ever wanted to do was to get back to Northern Fairyland."

Large tears suddenly started streaming down his face and I could tell by Emma's red cheeks she felt just as bad as I did for disbelieving them. Something also told me we'd not long met the Gaye Wood elves. But fairies? No way! Everyone knew fairies didn't exist!

"Watch this," said Will suddenly.

He held a plant pot containing a little soil beneath Clutterbutt's cheeks. A large tear splashed onto the earthy surface, and it began to move and bubble as though a miniature mole was mining for coal. Three seconds later and a shoot appeared quickly, followed by a dozen leaves and some purple-petalled flowers.

I stared in disbelief. How could that be?

"Supposing that you are real fairies just for one minute," said Emma hesitantly. "What's to stop you from using magic to get back to Northern Fairyland?"

Both Flumpkin and Clutterbutt groaned.

"Don't tell me you've forgotten, Emma," said Diana suddenly. "It was in the first book they ever did. Don't you remember – expelled from Northern Fairyland? The gate closed? The Ethereal Key? They have to find that before they can get back. Nothing else will work."

"That's right," wailed Clutterbutt. "We've spent the last three years searching. We've gone all over the world: New York, London, Paris; almost collapsed the Leaning Tower of Pisa; we've even been chased by polar bears! Every time we found even a hint of magical residue, we tried to investigate it; just in case it contained the Key. But never even a sniff."

It was a long time since I'd read the first book about Flumpkin and Clutterbutt but I could just about remember what he meant by magical residue. It was something left behind in the air after a strong spell had been cast. A bit like a smell or a sound or a fingerprint.

"That's why we were at your school," added Flumpkin. "We detected a magical residue there."

"So, it was you I saw, then" said I.

"Then we got spotted and had to create a diversion," said Clutterbutt, drying his eyes. "And now the Gaye Wood elves are on to us again, so we'll never be able to find out what it was."

"But how did you find your way here?" asked Emma. "I mean, of all the houses in Warren Hill you happened to choose this one."

"We – er – came across Diana's painting of us and your school records during our search in your school," said Flumpkin. "They mention how you formed the Flumpkin and Clutterbutt Appreciation Society two years ago and we thought you might like to – er – help us."

I suddenly felt my cheeks go warm. How dare they go through our records! But that wasn't the worst of it. The graffiti, the telephone mast - everything started to add up.

"There's a slight problem there," I snapped. "You've gone and gotten my friends expelled because of your stupid graffiti and daft antics – if you had any sense of decency, you'd go to the police and hand yourselves in!"

"What graffiti?" asked Clutterbutt looking puzzled.

My ears went hot.

"Oh, don't come all innocent with me," I shouted. Diana urgently shushed her finger to her lip so I lowered my voice and added, "I'm talking about the acorns on the town hall and the tree on the police station; and worst of all, no phones because some idiots have gone and blown up the telephone mast!"

Solemnly, Flumpkin pulled a long sliver of wood from his jeans pocket and declared, "I swear on my grandmother's wand I know nothing of what you are talking about."

A golden light emanated from the tip and glowed for a few seconds before fading.

"That's a fairy oath," whispered Diana. "You've got to believe him now. An oath of gold when truth is told! A wand is broken when lies are spoken!"

She was right. I made that rhyme up four years ago. In spite of the evidence to the contrary, though, I still couldn't believe it was Clutterbutt and Flumpkin. My overriding instinct was to hand them over to the Gaye Wood elves or whoever those crazy policemen were. They'd already admitted to the herd of wildebeest, and even if they weren't directly responsible for getting my friends suspended, I couldn't help but think they'd still done something to cause all the mayhem in the first place. I looked at Will, then Diana, then Emma. What were they thinking? Would they agree?

"We need to help you get back home," said Diana at last.

"But what are we going to do about this Ethereal Key?" asked Emma. "If you haven't noticed, three of us have been suspended."

Will suddenly smiled.

"I've just had an idea," he said. "It's going to be really risky but we've got to help them. I hereby declare the Clutterbutt and Flumpkin Appreciation Society is reformed and this is what we've got to do…"

CHAPTER FIVE – Flumpkin comes to School

The next day at the breakfast table with the smell of sizzling bacon in the air, I went over the plan in my head. If anyone other than Will had thought it out, I'd probably have refused point blank; as it was, I had serious misgivings and found myself seriously questioning Will's sanity. It was bad enough Flumpkin was accompanying me to school disguised as a foreign exchange student – but disguised as a girl, too?

"Flumpkin's too tall to borrow yours or my uniform," Will had told me. "Di's is the perfect fit, though, and she's not exactly going to need it for a while."

"And look on the bright side," Emma had added. "Those Gaye Wood elf cops won't suspect a girl to be looking for an ethereal key, either."

The others had seemingly accepted Flumpkin and Clutterbutt as real fairies but I was still unconvinced. True, we'd seen a few strange things happen; but for all I knew, it could all have been smoke and mirrors. My granddad had been a stage magician and doing pretend magic was not really all that difficult in my view.

A plate of bacon, egg and tomatoes suddenly appeared in front of me.

"Here you are, dear," said Mrs Jenkins, the housekeeper. "I'll bring you some tea in a mo."

Mrs Jenkins was a sprightly old lady in her sixties: very tall, prim and proper with a long pointy nose and tiny spectacles. She always came to cook for me whenever my father was away on business - which was like all the time.

I'd found his note when I'd gotten in. Gone chasing some asteroid fragments in Canada. Probably meant he'd be away for at least a week. Could be a month for all I cared.

The doorbell rang and I heard Mrs Jenkins answer it.

"Master Guy," she called. "There's a young lady called Britney here to see you – shall I show her in?"

"Go ahead," I called back.

Flumpkin walked into the room positively beaming. He'd done something to his hair to make it appear longer and twisted it into a 1960s beehive. As if that wasn't bad enough, he'd clearly put something down his blouse to make his chest appear larger and those fishnet stockings... I began to wish the previous year's school ban hadn't been lifted.

"Nice big house you've got," he said in a kind of American drawl; the kind that made Hollywood producers palm their foreheads in disbelief. "Whaddya think, buddy?"

"I think it's a nice house, too," I replied. "As for your accent, it's about as convincing as a rainbow-coloured snowflake and I'm not your buddy!"

"No, the disguise, silly!"

"I'm just glad you didn't opt to borrow one of Di's mini-skirts," I replied. "Have you had any breakfast?"

"Diana managed to sneak some toast into the back shed," he replied. "I must admit, I'm still a bit peckish though. My, that bacon looks tasty – do you mind?"

Before I could stop him, he's stuffed a whole three rashers into his mouth and wolfed them down. Mrs Jenkins then walked into the room, noticed my near-empty plate and remarked, "My word, Master Guy, you shouldn't bolt your food so, you'll get indigestion, or worse, choke yourself to death – now then," she added. "Will you be coming home for tea, or will you be going to one of your young lady-friends after school?"

"Probably go to Emma's," I replied.

She went back into the kitchen, muttering about not being appreciated, and Flumpkin belched so loudly I'm sure the crockery on the table rattled.

"Ah, that really hit the spot," he said. "Come on then, Guy, we really gotta get going if we're gonna find that Ethereal Key and I've got a really good feeling that today's the day."

Leaving the rest of my breakfast on the plate, we dashed out. It was a good twenty-minute walk to school, and normally I'd have taken the bus to Emma's first; however, this morning I opted to walk.

"So what are the others doing today?" I asked, wishing I could have been with them, too.

"Well," said Flumpkin, giving a flirtatious smile in the direction of a milkman driving a float. "After you and Emma left, we hit up on another idea."

I heard a screech of brakes and a sound of breaking glass in the background and hurried my pace.

"Your friend Diana didn't want to be in the house all day," Flumpkin went on, struggling to keep up with me in his high heels. "Apparently, her father doesn't know she's been suspended – so, they're actually going out to see if they can find this author chappie who wrote about us in the first place. What was it you called him? Mr Mystico?"

"What good'll that do?" I asked stepping back on the kerb as a police car rushed by with sirens wailing.

"Will thought this Mr Mystico might be able to throw some light on the situation having written all those books about us," said Flumpkin. "Clutterbutt thought it was a good idea, too, because there's a Level Ten spell which allows the caster to read people's thoughts from afar, and he thought maybe, just maybe, Mr Mystico is a very, very powerful wizard."

I doubted that very much but didn't let on. After all, it wasn't Mr Mystico who had made up the two fairy's names. I thought back to the time when he'd visited us in the primary school all those years ago. The school had just been struck by lightning, and all the computers were out, which was good for me because I really hated typing things on keyboards back then. Most of the kids had gone home, too, so it had just been me, Emma, Will, Diana and one or two others. My dad didn't work away at the time and things had been so much easier then.

"So what lessons have we got today?" Flumpkin asked casually.

"French, English and double biology," I replied. "Why do you ask?"

"Just need to plan a diversion so we can both get out. How does a six-foot-tall Eiffel Tower dressed in a tutu and dancing the Can-can sound?"

"Hold on," I said. "That wasn't part of the deal. The plan was, I bring you into school and pass you off as an exchange student so you can do your search. How you actually hunt for this Ethereal Key is your problem! Don't expect me to help; I've got to attend lessons so I can pass the notes and assignments on to my friends who've been suspended, remember?"

"And anyway," I added, holding up my finger and thumb in a near-complete circle. "I'm this far to getting suspended myself and if that happens, my lousy father'll probably send me back to boarding school like my brother and sister!"

A shudder went down my spine. Twice in the past I'd been sent to Saint Tremerwick's School for Boys and twice I ran away. The second time I'd taken a tent and camped out in the Snowdonia National Park for a week. The latter experience nearly killed me, and after a prolonged stay in hospital, my father agreed to let me go to Eleven Hills on condition I obtained good grades and didn't get into trouble.

"Look, Guy," said Flumpkin, fluttering his false eyelashes in a very annoying way. "Help me out, help me find this key and I promise you, Clutterbutt and I will be out of your hair in no time.

"I know you're still angry about what's happened to your friends but you never know, this graffiti business might be tied in with this author, too.

"From what I can gather, his books don't seem to sell that well, so he could have planned all this as a publicity stunt."

The gates of Eleven Hills came into view. I stopped and breathed deeply. Behind the fence, I noticed some purple-faced men in zookeeper uniforms slamming down their wildebeest dung-encrusted shovels in the back of a land rover.

"Alright then," I said, as their vehicle roared off. "I'll help you – but on one condition - you let me do the diversions."

"OK."

"And Flumpkin."

"Yes?"

"Don't do anything stupid that gets me expelled!"

CHAPTER SIX – Entropium Invertare

The first part of the morning passed with very little incident, although Mrs Creevely did call a special assembly first thing in the main hall.

"I don't care how long it takes," she said, banging the podium till the whole stage shook. "When I find the little terrorists who unleashed those beasts on the school yesterday, I will have them publically flogged and sent to juvenile penitentiary."

My unease about Flumpkin quickly evaporated, too, because the rest of the class seemed to accept him quite quickly. The fact he'd been quietly chuckling throughout Creevely's rant probably had something to do with it because that sort of thing quickly got you respect in Eleven Hills High. Either that or an instant suspension if caught.

Things started to get a little out of hand after English, though. It began when Mr Dobson held me back after class.

"I just want to tell you," he said, rubbing his bushy grey eyebrows. "I'm really, really sorry that your friends got suspended, and I don't believe for one moment that anyone from Eleven Hills was responsible for the graffiti or blowing up the mobile phone mast."

I hurried out of the classroom afterwards, intending to catch up with Flumpkin. Down the corridor, I dashed where I could see him chatting to Terry Smythers-McCoy. I quickened my pace but I collided with what felt like a living, breathing brick wall.

"Watch where you're going, Foulkstone," snapped a thick accented voice and my heart sank.

Before me stood Vinny Kruger, a full six feet tall and almost the same widthways. His blue eyes stared cold, and his mousy brown hair was cropped to a Number Two.

"You were in my 'hood last night, weren't you, Foulkstone," he said suddenly.

"That's right," I replied. "I went to take Diana some work."

"Well," he said with a menacing snarl. "If I ever see you there again, I'll make you sorry you were ever born. In fact, if I'm feeling bored, I might even wait for you after school…"

He pushed past me suddenly and stormed off.

"I saw that. Do you want me to have a word with Alfie Leung?"

A small second-year with a thick mop of greasy blond hair appeared out of nowhere. I nodded my head and handed her a fifty-pound note from my pocket.

"No violence, mind," I added, before she scurried off. "Just the usual friendly persuasion."

The trouble with Vinny was he kept forgetting he wasn't supposed to hassle me and had to be reminded every so often. The only person who could do that was Alfie Leung, the school's resident karate black belt. It had to be low key, friendly persuasion with no violence though, in case any questions were asked. Needless to say, putting contracts out on fellow students if found out would have meant expulsion and a one-way ticket to Tremerwick's.

"I don't believe you just did that," said a female voice with an annoyingly unAmerican accent behind me.

I span around. Flumpkin looked at me with his eyebrows raised.

"You know," he said. "One day, you'll have to fight a battle and there'll be no one there to fight it for you – what'll you do then, Mr Moneybags?"

"It's alright for you to say that," I snapped back. "You're just a fairy tale character. You can hide in your book. I've got to survive in the real world."

Flumpkin's cheeks went bright red and for a moment, he looked as though he was about to burst into tears.

"The sooner I find this Ethereal Key," he hissed, still in his female voice. "The sooner I can get back into the real world. Don't forget your side of the bargain, Guy. Get me that diversion and I'll get out of your hair and your conscience!"

Flumpkin stormed off, and once again, I felt bad inside. He must have been really mad at me because, in the biology practical, he teamed up with Terry Smythers-McCoy.

The room where we were was very old-fashioned with long black benches, sinks and gas taps. On one side was a large window and a small date palm looking out towards the tennis courts; the back wall was full of colourful posters depicting hearts, lungs and kidneys; and the wall opposite the window had shelves and cupboards stacked with equipment and specimen jars containing dead frogs, worms, rats, a particularly large octopus and other things too grotesque to mention.

Terry Smithers-McCoy took great joy in taunting me over Flumpkin.

"She's not so fond of you now, is she, Fawksey," he sneered, getting a microscope and a dissecting kit. "And do you know what? There's this brilliant new Robin and Ryan film at the cinema tonight. I doubt they have them in America but I'm sure she'll find them truly inspirational!"

"I'm sure you'll find her very *truly* inspirational, too," I answered with a sardonic grin.

In spite of this, I still felt bad inside about the way I'd spoken to Flumpkin. Slowly I hatched my plan. Miss Valentino, the class teacher, walked past me, her long black hair swaying rhythmically. Quickly, I seized my chance.

"'Scuse me, Miss Valentino," I said, raising my hand. "I've just remembered, I haven't taken Fru – I mean, Britney to the Headmistress for her introductory talk; is it OK to take her now?"

"Do you think I was-a born yesterday?" said the teacher with a flash of her brown eyes. "The last time I let you leave-a my class, you were caught smoking in the toilets."

Flumpkin looked over at me in disgust and Terry Smythers-McCoy sniggered. I couldn't believe Miss Valentino still remembered what was probably my one and only ever minor indiscretion. Once! Just the once in Year 8, I'd tried a cigarette out of curiosity! Never again! It wasn't as though I made a habit of it like some people in my class. Take Toby 'Ten Chimneys' Riley cutting slices of onion by the date palm for example; he was always nipping out of school in the dinner break.

"I'm feeling a bit dizzy," I tried again five minutes later. "Could I go see the nurse?"

"No, sit down and rest for five-a minutes!" snapped Miss Valentino.

Flumpkin looked at me and shook his head. I could tell by the wobble in his beehive hairdo he wasn't impressed. There was nothing for it – I'd have to do the old fingers down the back of the throat and vomit trick. Suddenly, Flumpkin produced a thin sliver of wood – the same one he'd sworn an oath on the previous night.

"No, don't," I mouthed in his direction with a nightmare vision of Tremerwick Towers coming to mind.

Too late. He gave it a few sweeps and mouthed a silent incantation. Fortunately. Nothing happened.

I held my hands out and looked at him with what I hoped was a quizzical expression. He smiled. Suddenly there was a strangled scream, and Toby Riley started staggering about, clutching at his collar. Outside in the corridor, the peace was disturbed by a sudden cacophony of noise and screaming. Several specimen jars on the shelf opposite the window exploded, and from one of these there emerged the large badly-decomposed octopus, which promptly began an eight-legged, break-dance routine.

"Everybody, get-a da hell outta here," squealed Miss Valentino valiantly, fending off the octopus with her Antonio Dachia handbag. The rest of the class bar Toby complied with a cacophonous clatter of chairs, a raucous rumble of feet and a scattering of notepaper. Toby meanwhile was still clutching at his collar and turning blue in the face. I realised to my horror several slithering green snake-like appendages had sprouted from out of the palm by the window. One of these had wrapped itself round Toby's neck and another was inching stealthily towards his waist.

"Come on, Flumpkin," I said, vaulting over the bench and picking up a sharp dissecting knife. "Don't just stand there and gawp – help me out here!"

Even though the blade was a small one, it cut through the green appendage like a knife through butter. The plant immediately released Toby and he fell to the floor gasping.

The date palm immediately turned its attention to me. With a gibbering sound, one of its appendages whipped across my face, and I tasted blood, a second one caught my wrist in a vice-like grip and pulled me closer.

Outside in the corridor, the fire bell hammered away – it was then I noticed a bottle of laboratory alcohol on Toby's desk.

"Do it," gasped Flumpkin, who'd been similarly caught and was trying to free both his arms from the green beast.

My rugby training kicked in. With all the speed I could muster, I flung the bottle contents at the plant with my free hand and the liquid ran down its woody stem and leaves.

Toby meanwhile staggered up, ripped the centre pages out of his note-book and lit them with a Bunsen burner.

"Die, biatch!" he snarled, throwing the flaming missile at the vexatious vegetable.

With a high-pitched squeal, it erupted into flames and the grip of its appendages slackened.

"Come on, boys," said Mrs Valentino standing by the remains of the zombie octopus and wiping her brow. "Let's-a get to the fire assembly point, outside."

All along the corridor, there were signs of chaos: Twittering baby chicks were streaming out of the cookery class leaving broken eggshells in their wake; the ghost of William Shakespeare was doing a re-enactment of Hamlet to empty desks in the English class; and in the history room, a highwayman was blowing bubblegum and trying to fathom out how to work a mobile phone.

We were joined by a crowd of traumatised fifth-years and managed to lose Toby and Miss Valentino in the main corridor near the main hall.

"What on earth did you do?" I whispered to Flumpkin.

"Entropium Invertare," he whispered, looking around nervously. "Otherwise known as a chaos grenade – though how it got out of hand like this, I really don't know."

"No, really?" I said sarcastically.

"No, you don't understand, to have gone the way it did, there's got to be evil in the air and that evil wasn't here yesterday."

Flumpkin stopped suddenly.

"That door," he said, pointing at some very old-looking oak panelling in an alcove. "Where does it lead to?"

To be honest, it wasn't a door I had noticed before. The wood looked warped and battered and the varnish looked faded.

"It probably leads to the stage in the main hall," I replied, trying to open it. "Come on, we'd better get to the assembly point."

"Too late, they're here," whispered Flumpkin jumping back into the alcove.

I peered around the corner and immediately noticed the two motorcycle cops making their way through the crowds. They were bound to see us when they drew level. Being caught red-handed with an escaped lunatic wasn't going to do me any favours right now, especially in light of recent events and self-preservation took over.

"Flumpkin," I hissed. "Are you able to open that door?"

CHAPTER SEVEN – Behind the Door

"Invisible key," hissed Flumpkin holding up his finger and thumb.

Like a mime artist, he lowered his finger and thumb level with the lock and turned his wrist. It clicked and I immediately turned the polished brass knob.

The door opened with an ominous creak and beyond there was just darkness. We didn't mind though, and quickly passed through and closed the door behind us.

"Just in case," whispered Flumpkin, turning his imaginary key in the lock once again and sealing us in. Watching him reminded me of my grandfather. He'd been a stage magician when he was alive and had done a similar trick with a pair of handcuffs. With him though, I knew it had all been smoke and mirrors. At least I thought I knew. My grandfather had disappeared years ago whilst on a hiking trip in the Himalayas and was assumed dead.

The surroundings began to take shape and I realised we were in an old corridor. Several large assegais and Zulu shields stacked against the wall looked vaguely familiar, and I was reminded of a dance the rugby team had done for the Christmas concert in my first year at Eleven Hills. We walked down the corridor and saw other props, too: masks the size of dustbin lids; Viking costumes; and even an old engine block.

"Are you sure this corridor leads to the stage?" Flumpkin whispered after two minutes.

"I think so," I replied.

Just then, it opened up into a much larger corridor running perpendicular to the one we were in. Though dimly lit, I could see the dirty grey plaster on the wall was cracked and coming away in places to reveal old fashioned brickwork beneath.

Openings appeared at regular intervals in the gloom, some with doors and some with the remnants of doors. We looked behind one and saw a large tatty classroom with old-fashioned wooden desks and blackboards. The windows had long since been bricked up. I realised we were in a disused part of the school.

"You know," said Flumpkin. "The aura of magic is actually a lot stronger around here than it is in the modern part of your school; I think we should start looking for the Ethereal key in the classrooms around here, now."

"What exactly are we looking for?" I asked. "Is it like a golden key floating in the air?"

Flumpkin laughed and his eyes lit up.

"Not quite, have you ever seen the shimmering haze rising up from a tarmac road on a really sunny day?"

I nodded.

"It's just like that, only it swirls like a cloud and you actually have to reach into it to pull out the Ethereal key."

Flumpkin's description reminded me of the last time I'd seen Mr Mystico.

You couldn't have missed him really. Tall, black combed-back hair, droopy, oiled black moustache and a permanent grin. He'd come to visit us at Di's (fortunately, her dad had been working at the time) to say thank you for trying to get more people to read his books in school.

"It doesn't really matter what the Ethereal key looks like," he told us at the time. "That's why I called it 'ethereal' because it implies a lack of shape and substance. No, what is actually important is the journey Clutterbutt and Flumpkin undertake to find the key."

"Flumpkin?" I asked.

"Umm?"

"How did you manage to survive searching for the key for the last three years without any money or home to go to?"

"Ways and means," Flumpkin replied. "Ways and means – for example, we disguised ourselves as sailors and went to America in a nuclear submarine and whilst we were there we worked on a cattle ranch and even sold trinkets on an Indian reservation."

"None of that was in the books," I said.

"Well, it wouldn't be.

"What you've got to understand, Guy, is that Clutterbutt and I are most definitely not two-dimensional creatures from a fairy story, though from what Diana was saying last night, your Mr Mystico seems to have gotten quite a few things right about us.

"You see, before we got thrown out of Northern Fairyland, we were both pages in the court of Merry Queen Mabiley the Third and had we stayed there, we'd probably have been made knight protectors by now."

"What's a knight protector?" I asked.

"Have you ever wondered why there are no witches and werewolves in your world?"

"Er, because they don't exist," I replied.

"No, it's because the knight protectors from our world sometimes come to this one and hunt them down to protect you."

"Do they kill them?" I asked.

"Not if they can avoid it. Once they capture them, they send them to various reservations in Northern and Southern Fairyland – believe me, they're a lot happier there and they make a great tourist attraction, too.

"What, tourists from this world?" I asked.

"There's been the occasional one in the past, but mostly they come from places like Lilliput or Xanadu or Atlantis."

"Those places really exist?"

Flumpkin grinned.

"Come on, Guy, what do you think?" he asked.

I was about to ask him another question when I heard footsteps in the corridor. Flumpkin heard them too because he shushed his finger to his lips. Slowly, we ducked behind an old battered desk.

Ten seconds later, a shadowy figure swept by beyond the door. Stealthily, we crept out like mice on a midnight pantry raid in a cattery full of half-starved moggies and made our way into the corridor. We continued following the shadowy figure for a good minute or two and then, just beyond the bust of a long-forgotten headmaster, we saw her turn a key and disappear.

Quickly, we made our way to the spot and noticed a door similar to the one we'd originally come through. I looked through the keyhole and had a shock. It was Mrs Creevely's office and she was about to speak into a large microphone.

"Teachers and pupils," she said, her voice echoing off the walls and carrying around the whole school. "The – ah – fire drill is now over but due to unforeseen circumstances we must now close the school for the afternoon.

"In accordance with school fire policies, all class teachers must tick the children off their registers as they leave through the gates. Anyone who is left on site, a thorough search must be conducted for them."

A muffled cheer echoed down the dark corridor.

"We really better had been going," I whispered.

"Agreed," whispered Flumpkin. "But I think we should come back here tonight and carry on our search – I feel we're getting really close."

CHAPTER EIGHT – Comparing Notes

Once we'd been ticked off on the register and allowed to leave Flumpkin put an invisibility charm over us.

"Just in case those elves appear again," he said.

It was a good thing he did, too, because waiting just a minute down the road in the entrance to Warren Hill Park was Vinny Kruger and a gang of his pals.

"Keep your eyes peeled for him, lads," he said, looking around with a malevolent glint in his eye. "He's the short guy with the really short blond hair – he was hanging round earlier with a really ugly-looking girl in fishnets and a ridiculously retro beehive."

"I've changed my mind about what I said earlier," whispered Flumpkin into my ear. "You should've paid that Alfie Leung fellow to belt him with a custard tart. Preferably one made with a permanent flatulence hex – by the way," he added, yanking me back by the scruff of the neck as I went to cross the road. "Don't forget the cars can't see you so don't expect them to slow down for you!"

We made our way home and entered the house through the garage at the side. As far as garages went, it was quite a large one and contained all three of my father's pride and joys: a metallic blue Range Rover; a shiny black Porsche; and a 1960s silver Mercedes he sometimes took to classic car shows with my brother and sister. Never with me, though.

"Nice cars," remarked Flumpkin. "Now if you took one of those to school you wouldn't need to worry about getting ambushed on the way home."

"Great idea," I replied with a sardonic raise of my eyebrows. "Remind me again in another three years when I'm allowed to drive."

A vision of a black limousine with some rather rude words spray-painted on it crystallised in my mind's eye as I thought of the first and last time the High Mayor of Manchester visited Eleven Hills High.

"Honestly though," Flumpkin went on. "You've got to do something about that Vinny fellow because sooner or later he's going to get you alone – what'll you do then? Wave a fifty-pound note in his face? From the way he looked this afternoon you could've waved the crown jewels in his face and he'd probably have rammed them down your throat."

I looked at Flumpkin and smiled.

"Unless you know someone who can give me a five-minute intensive course in every single martial art under the sun, that's probably going to be my only choice."

Deep down, I knew Flumpkin was absolutely right. Sometimes you could hit a bully and they'd never bother you again. Other times, you'd hit them and they'd come back afterwards for more. Either way, you ended up fighting and with that came the risk of expulsion and for me at least, resumption of my academic career in Tremerwick Towers away from my friends was not an option I wanted to risk.

"Tell you what," said Flumpkin. "I'm going to teach you a simple Level One spell you can use to protect yourself; it's called an – ah – psychic block."

"What on earth's that?" I asked.

"Watch me!"

With a loud shout, he stepped forward onto his right foot and at the same time extended his right arm so the flat of his hand was pointing outwards with his body side-on.

"And that'll really work?" I said incredulously.

"Fairy's honour!" replied Flumpkin putting his other hand round his back. "But you've got to make the shout come right from the back of your lungs and you've got to push your hand in the direction of your attacker's face to direct the spell!"

I was still practising the spell with Flumpkin when the others arrived an hour or so later. Clutterbutt was carrying a laptop computer under his arm and looking pleased as punch. Will, Emma and Di, on the other hand, were looking at him as though he was something rather unpleasant they'd found on the end of their shoes.

"This idiot went and broke into Mr Mystico's flat!" declared Will.

"And nicked his laptop!" added Di.

"It was all in a good cause," assured Clutterbutt. "Anyway, he's disappeared so it's not really stealing – it's more like borrowing; that's to say…"

"Hold on," I said. "Did you just say disappeared?"

Emma placed a photocopied newspaper clip in front of me.

It read:

Mystery of Failed Author's Disappearance Deepens

Police were last night still baffled by the apparent disappearance of the failed children's author Melvyn Mystico who hasn't been seen now for the last six months. A former ringmaster at Anna Ramsbottom's Family Circus, he is reasonably well known around Manchester for writing subversive children's literature many of which have now been banned from the city libraries under the Supreme City Council's Putting Realism into Literature Campaign…

Where could he have gone to, I wondered. Was it in any way connected with the appearance of Flumpkin and Clutterbutt? Had he perhaps been kidnapped by the Gaye Wood elves? There was very little additional information in the article save some neighbour suggesting Mr Mystico had been very depressed recently because of the poor sales of his books.

"What else did you find out?" I asked.

"Nothing much really," replied Will. "His address wasn't in the telephone directory but I still had his card from the last time we saw him." He laughed, then added, "Those flats where he lived made Concrete Close look like the Riviera!"

Di frowned at him.

"We told Clutterbutt not to go into his flat," she went on, turning to Clutterbutt and glaring at him. "But he insisted, saying we were only trying to help which made it alright."

"We found out a bit more there, too," said Clutterbutt, his eyes shining. From down the back of his trousers, he produced a large family album.

Emma looked mortified.

"You stole that, too?" she said with a gasp.

"Not stole, bo-rrowed," said Clutterbutt, flicking the album open. I noticed a black and white photograph of an elderly gentleman in a suit holding a rabbit above a top hat.

"Don't you see," he went on excitedly. "This is a photograph of Mr Mystico's grandfather. It says here he was a magician which just goes to prove my theory that Mr Mystico is a very powerful wizard and can do Level Ten spells because if there's one thing we fairies know, magic tends to skip a generation in people."

"It doesn't prove anything," I said, looking over at Di, who was twiddling her index finger above her eyebrow. "Stage magicians don't do proper magic, it's all smoke and mirrors and I ought to know because my grandfather was one, too."

His picture was still on our mantelpiece. Blue eyes, white beard, a scar on his left cheek and long grey hair like an aging heavy rock star. Up in the attic, there was a box full of ancient props my grandfather had left behind, too: wands, a black coat with sleeve-pockets; a top hat you could put your hand through; a small table filled with secret compartments. These were just some of the things I'd pulled out and played with when I was about eleven but now they had very little interest to me.

"So did you two find anything at school?" asked Will.

"A little," I replied and proceeded to tell everyone about the hidden corridor from the moment we saw the Gaye Wood elves to the moment we saw Creevely in her office.

"There's something else," added Flumpkin when I'd finished. "I tried a chaos spell earlier and it misfired, pretty dangerously, too – I think there's some sort of evil presence in the school that caused it – I don't know why, it's just a feeling I've got."

Emma laughed.

"There's been an evil presence in Eleven Hills High for the last two years," she said.

"You don't understand," said Flumpkin. "Clutterbutt and I did a chaos spell yesterday in your school and that pretty much worked OK. We both thought of a small herd of Wildebeest and they materialised. This morning, I thought of the plant growing legs and scurrying out of the classroom, instead, it tried to strangle someone."

We continued talking about the misfired spell for sometime, trying to work out what might have happened. I even joked Creevely might have started a witches coven which brought a frown from Flumpkin.

"That's not funny at all," he said.

"Got it," said Emma suddenly. "It's those Gaye Woode elves! They're obviously not proper policemen. I could tell by their shoes. They must have been hanging about. How else would they have gotten to school so quickly once the fire alarm went?"

Something else clicked in my head – the police motorbikes I'd seen yesterday going to school after the wildebeest incident – it had to be them.

"Why exactly are those elves after you?" I asked the two fairies.

"To be honest, we never stopped to find out," replied Clutterbutt. "Fairies and elves never did see eye to eye."

"But it does make sense, I suppose," said Di. "The elves hadn't been to our school before the wildebeest incident so perhaps they anticipated you'd return and went and put some sort of anti-magic hex on the school – you know, like they did at the cinema in 'Flumpkin and Clutterbutt visit London' when you got chased by the popcorn stands."

"I'd forgotten that," said Clutterbutt with a grin.

"You mean it actually happened?" said Di.

"We're still both wanted for high treason if that's what you mean," said Flumpkin. "But it seems a bit extreme when all we did was hide in the Houses of Parliament and accidentally blow up a few of the toilet seats in the process."

"And it was the summer recess," added Clutterbutt. "So, no one actually got hurt."

Will gave an impatient wave of his hand.

"This is getting us nowhere," he said. "We still haven't found this Ethereal Key and we're still no closer to finding Mr Mystico, either."

"But that's where you're wrong and what I've been trying to tell you," said Clutterbutt, eagerly holding up the laptop. "There's bound to be a few clues in this computery-whatsit-thing. He might have even got a draft of his final Flumpkin and Clutterbutt novel which tells us where we can find the key."

"It's worth a look," I said, taking it from him and placing it on the table. However, when I opened it up and pressed the on button, all I got was a request for a password.

"Here's what I think we should do," said Will. "Me and Di need to run a bit more research on the internet. I think we might be able to find Mr Mystico in one of the local circuses.

Think about it, he's not exactly been that successful as an author so maybe he's gone back to his old job.

"Also," he went on. "I might be able to take the hard drive out of Mr Mystico's PC and read it from another PC if I'm lucky and there's no back-end encryption. Di, you've got a hard-drive reader at home, can we take it to your place?"

Di nodded.

"What about us?" said Emma.

"I think the rest of you need to go back to school and carry on searching through this old corridor place for the key. That way we're tackling the problem from two angles. One of us is bound to come up with something sooner or later."

"He's a clever fellow that friend of yours," said Flumpkin a little later as Di and Will left through my front gate. "I'm really glad we've bumped into the Clutterbutt and Flumpkin Appreciation Society – no one else would have done so much for us."

I ordered a couple of pizzas for tea. Flumpkin, Emma and I shared a twelve inch ham and sweetcorn whilst Clutterbutt managed to put away two twelve-inch pizzas, each with a prawn, anchovy, onion, olive and salami topping.

He belched loudly and relaxed on the leather sofa in the front room with his feet on a large pouffe. Without asking, he picked up the remote and put the large wall-mounted flatscreen on.

"I've always wanted one of these," he said, flicking through the channels and stopping on a weather forecast. "Look at this for example, it's amazing how you humans can spend so much time talking about something as mundane as the weather…"

"… and now as if the massive mobile phone outage isn't enough," said the weather girl, oblivious to her audience. "We have some rather unusual band patterns developing over Manchester. These isobars are so tight in fact that in the next twenty-four hours or so we could be seeing anything from hail to monsoon to blizzards; a bit of midsummer madness with the satellite, no doubt…"

"Come on, Clutterbutt," said Flumpkin, switching off the flatscreen with a flick of his wand. "We've got to get back to searching for the Key."

"Don't do that," snapped Clutterbutt, pulling his own wand out in a flash.

Flumpkin span on his foot, wand crackling at the ready. An oil painting of my father, brother and sister flew off the wall.

"DON'T YOU DARE HAVE A WAND FIGHT IN HERE," I said in a loud voice.

"Sorry," said Clutterbutt, putting it back in his pocket with big puppy-dog eyes. "But I'm really tired, so tired in fact, I could sleep for a week, and I really don't fancy walking to your school – have you seen the weather outside?"

Outside the window, the sky had turned black. There was a sudden clap of thunder, and rain started coming down in buckets, rat-a-tatting on the windows and roof. It was the stair-rail kind of rain. The kind that soaked you on the way down, then bounced up off the ground and soaked you again on the way up.

"What we really need," said Flumpkin looking in the direction of the garage corridor, "is a car to take us to your school, now I wonder where we could get a car?"

"Forget it," I snapped. "I'll call a taxi."

"Too conspicuous," said Clutterbutt as several more crashes of thunder sounded outside and the intensity of the rat-a-tat-tatting increased.

I picked up the landline phone anyway but it was dead.

"Your dad's golfing umbrella," suggested Emma. "We could use that, maybe."

"Not with thunder and lightning," I replied. "We'd be frazzled in a flash."

"Come on, Guy," said Flumpkin. "I know you're too young to drive but I'm a fairly accomplished driver, even if I may say so myself. I'll even drive the car if you like. I've always wanted to drive a Mercedes."

"Oh no you won't," I retorted, seeing visions of St Tremerwick's grey towers in my mind's eye. "I haven't forgotten that bit in the book where you borrowed that London cab and it ended up on the roof of Buckingham Palace!"

"What about the bit where he chased the Mona Lisa through Paris," said Clutterbutt. "He drove OK then, and if you're worried about being found out, it's only a Level Two spell that's needed to change the number plate. Your dad'll never know. I'll even put back the milometer reading for you."

"It's not a bad idea," said Emma, rubbing my shoulder. "And just think, if we find this Ethereal Key, they'll be able to get themselves home tonight."

That was persuasion enough. Five minutes later, I was in the back of my dad's Merc with Emma. Flumpkin was driving, honking the horn and Clutterbutt was busy trying to get a tune out of the old radio. The rain was still rat-a-tat-tatting on the car roof and every so often, a bright flash of thunder lit the now dark sky. Surprising, really, because it was only a half-past-six.

"Nearly there," said Flumpkin, swerving so as not to avoid a massive puddle and drenching a dozen or so people inside a bus shelter in the process.

"Uh-oh," said Clutterbutt, suddenly, as we neared the school.

"What is it?"

I looked ahead in the direction of his pointing finger and, just beside the open school gates, saw two police motorcycles parked ahead.

CHAPTER NINE – The Two Witches

"Drive on!" I hissed.

"No need," said Clutterbutt, producing his wand. Then giving it a slight swish, he whispered, "Invisible carriage!"

A slight shiver ran down my spine.

"What's he done?" asked Emma with a shudder.

"Put us into stealth mode," said Flumpkin with his eyes still on the road. "Now if you don't mind, I'm just going to do a little test – hold on to your seats everyone!"

There was a squeal of brakes and I was thrown back into my seat. Clutterbutt gave a whoop of delight and the large school building blurred into a dizzying kaleidoscope. A split second later, we were heading back the way we came.

"Er, Flumpkin," I said, noticing a set of oncoming headlights. "We're on the wrong side of the road."

"No probs," came the reply and a second later, I was thrown back into my seat as the Mercedes accelerated forward.

"Flumpkin!" I shouted, more worried for the car than myself.

"Relax!"

Closing my eyes and gritting my teeth, I felt Emma clutching my arm; her nails digging into my flesh. Some people say when faced with certain death, your whole life flashes before your eyes. All I could think of was a waltzer ride we'd shared some weeks previously at one of the local fairs – long before Clutterbutt and Flumpkin invaded our lives.

There was a slight lurch to the left and mercifully no impact; then another screech of brakes followed by another spinning sensation.

"Nice work!" said Clutterbutt, sounding like an art teacher praising a particularly perfect painting. "She didn't see us at all."

"What do you mean, nice work?" I spluttered. "You nearly killed us!"

"I had to test the spell," muttered Flumpkin, slowing down the car and approaching the school gates. "Actually," he added in a louder voice. "I think I saw a slight flicker in the old lady's eyes just as we passed her, so maybe we're still displaying a shadow. Could you just re-do the spell, Clutterbutt, just to be on the safe side."

Clutterbutt repeated the spell and we came to a halt in the teachers' car park. It was strange to see it so empty in the cold, wet gloom of the night. I was reminded by my now pounding heartbeat I hadn't exactly ever done anything like this before.

The rain stopped and I helped a very pale-looking Emma out of the car. We both marvelled at how the now-invisible door when open, revealed the Mercedes's grey leather upholstery seemingly floating above the tarmac. In some strange way, it enviously reminded me of the old advent calendars my brother and sister used to get every run up to Christmas when they returned from boarding school.

"They could have parked it a bit better," Emma remarked, looking at the white dividing line running beneath where the car should have been.

"As if anyone's going to notice it," grinned Flumpkin, getting out his side. "Now," he added. "Those elves are still about, no doubt – so another invisibility charm on us, too, is in order, here."

"You'd better do the honours," said Clutterbutt. "My wand's a bit droopy after those last two spells; it's never had to hide a Merc before and I think I've tired it out a bit."

"No probs."

Flumpkin cast the charm and I felt a slight tingle down my back. The others were still visible to me and I was reminded of earlier in the day when we'd passed Vinny and his cronies. Back then I'd been able to see Flumpkin, just as now, but I'd accepted it without question. Emma, however, was more curious.

"If we're invisible, how come we can see each other?" she asked. Then noticing an empty space where the car stood, added, "And how come the car is still invisible?"

"They're different spells, that's why," said Flumpkin. "You've got to remember, a car is not a living thing whereas we are – can you imagine how weird it would be if the car could actually see us and decided to follow us into the school?"

"It'd be fun, though, wouldn't it?" grinned Clutterbutt, pulling his wand out and raising it over the Merc.

"Don't you even dare," I retorted with a feral snarl.

"Only kidding!"

We made our way to the main entrance. The door was unlocked so Flumpkin didn't need to use his invisible key. Although the corridor was dark, we could see a light and hear muffled voices from the direction of Mrs Creevely's office.

"Wonder what the old hag's doing?" whispered Emma.

"Don't call people 'hags'," whispered Clutterbutt, handing out torches. "It's not nice; especially when you've seen one in real life."

"With a bit of luck she might have the elves with her," I suggested.

We moved on. The door to the old corridor was locked; however, the invisible key trick worked as it had done before. Once inside and in the torchlight, Emma looked in disgust at the old stage props and I could tell her loathing for Mrs Creevely had just gone up another notch. Not least because a pale pink spangly outfit lay in a crumpled heap on the floor – the very same one she'd worn in a dance act on stage during our second-year Christmas concert.

"It might be an idea to split up," said Flumpkin when we got to the bit where the corridor widened. "Guy, you take the left with Clutterbutt, Emma, you come with me. Remember, we're looking for a swirly, shimmery, hazy thing."

"Could I go with Guy, instead?" whispered Emma.

"No, best do it my way," whispered Flumpkin, producing his wand. "Just in case we need protection."

I watched them both disappear into the darkness. A chill draft emanating from a large crack in the mouldering plaster caused a shiver to run down my spine. For a brief second, I wished we were in Concrete Close instead. At least we knew what to look out for, there.

"Well, let's get on our way, then," said Clutterbutt in a hesitant voice.

As we moved, it felt as though the dark was closing in on us: buffeting, choking, strangling, and swallowing up the meagre torchlight like some voracious vampire starved for a thousand years of its prey. We followed the corridor to a set of stone stairs barely visible within a gloomy recess. These went upwards, twisting and turning like a snake before coming to a dead end in the shape of a bricked-up wall. Clutterbutt put his ear to the crumbling red brickwork as though listening for some unknown activity then shook his head.

"Nothing here," he whispered.

We retraced our steps back into the corridor and presently came across a small disused assembly hall festooned with cobwebs containing a small stage and low-lying seating-benches. Opposite this was a class containing the rusting hulks of mechanical lathes, drills and saws and in a corner on a dust-covered table, several half-finished wooden boats looking as though they were embarking on some endless voyage into eternity.

"There's evil in this place," whispered Clutterbutt suddenly. "Can you feel it?"

I nodded my head. It was hard to describe; almost like some half-starved rat gnawing away at my stomach and a constant high-pitch tinkling sound in my ears. We followed the sound and it took us straight back into the cobweb-festooned assembly hall.

Clutterbutt suddenly gripped my arm and pointed with his torch.

"Can you see it?" he whispered.

There in the torchlight, barely visible by the steps leading to the stage, a shimmering mass with a jet black lustre not too dissimilar to freshly-cut coal pulsated like the heart of an enormous beast. Somewhere deep inside me, a voice screamed a warning, and without another word, I seized Clutterbutt's torch and switched it off.

"What did you do that...?" he began.

Before he could finish, an ominous creak and two figures climbed onto the stage through what looked like a trap-door in the middle. In spite of the invisibility charm, we immediately ducked behind the door and retreated into the old woodwork classroom. Scared least my pounding heart gave us both away, I shrank into the cold metallic caress of one of the old rusting pieces of machinery. Outside, the two figures began talking. The first voice was gravelly and high-pitched and said:

"Tell me, good Helga, how can it be;

"Magyck is now so widespread and free.

"Before in my world there was naught but despair,

"But now I feel enchantments so thick in the air.

"Could it be some savant has paved us the way

"And brought our salvation yet closer today?

"And tell me also, good Helga, what must we do

"To grow this good fortune and see it all through?"

A similar ancient-sounding voice replied:

"We must bring the last vessel here one more day hence;

"At knifepoint if necessary to make him see sense.

"Then together, the gatekeeper and he;

"And the one, once entombed in a book but now free,

"Will complete the circle with a red river of wine;

"And free up the magyck and roll back the time.

"The tempest to follow will pave us the way;

"And free all our kind for many a day.

"Chaos will abide and the world will be ours.

"And all will then bow to our invincible powers."

The air surrounding us began to crackle and the hairs on my arms stood on end. Clutterbutt's teeth were knocking together as well; not surprising really, the voice deep inside me was saying: "get out, get out" and every sinew in my body was taut like cheese wire. Fortunately, showing no sign they'd heard him, the two old ladies passed us by and carried on down the corridor.

I looked into Clutterbutt's eyes. They were wide with fear and his mouth was now moving as if he was trying to say something.

"W-w-w-w-witches," he managed at last.

"Come off it," I whispered. "There's no such thing."

"Y-y-y-you said that about fairies, too – why do you have to be in denial all the time?"

"OK then," I said, remembering something Flumpkin had said earlier. "Supposing for one minute they are, surely your knight protectors would have caught them and sent them to one of your tourist parks."

"Y-y-you can't always count on that! Come on, we'd better warn the others."

Following in the footsteps of the two old ladies, we hurried down the corridor, going as stealthily as we could. It wasn't easy in the dark, but fortunately we knew there weren't many obstacles in the way. I just hoped beyond all hope that the old ladies would turn off into the corridor leading to the old stage props and allow us to pass them by.

Unfortunately, they didn't. We caught up with them just as they walked past it, heading in the direction of Creevely's office. Suddenly, they stopped. Had they heard us? Ducking behind a plinth, I peered around. Closer up, they looked hideous in the darkness with their black cloaks, unkempt greasy grey hair and shrivelled hands. What surprised me most of all was their total lack of pointy hats. What if they really were witches though? Even if they weren't, what if they were working with the Gaye wood elves and discovered Emma and Flumpkin further up the corridor?

In desperation, I tore a chunk of crumbling plaster from the wall and hurled it down the narrow corridor in the direction of the stage props. It made a terrible racket and the echo seemed to resonate in my bones as well as against the walls.

The first old lady immediately spoke out: "By the teeth rotting in my gums, is it the gatekeeper this way comes?"

There was a silence and I held my breath. Clutterbutt stood rigidly still, too.

The second old lady cursed and snarled: "By the filth beneath my nails and the most horrid banshee wails, if thou won't answer me now, I'll spin a hex and make thee a cow!"

Two seconds later, she pulled out a crooked black stick from beneath her cloak and gave it a swish in the direction of the props corridor. Green sparks flew from the tip causing the whole corridor to be illuminated in a horrible fluorescent green glow. The air crackled and the voice inside me screamed louder. The whole corridor vibrated in a way that made more lumps of plaster fall from the walls. Any doubts I'd had about these two ladies being witches evaporated in an instant.

The next second, Clutterbutt put his thumb to his nose and moved his lips. A loud resonant "Mooooo!" came from the direction the witch had cast her spell in and they both rushed down the narrow passageway in the direction of the stage props to investigate; their black cloaks swishing behind them.

"Come on," hissed Clutterbutt.

We both scurried past the exit the witches had taken and ran in the direction of Creevely's office. A couple of minutes later, we saw torchlight and heard low whispers. A second later, the torch went out.

"It's OK, it's only us," I whispered.

The torch went back on with a click, and for an instant, I was blinded. Quickly, Clutterbutt explained to the others what had happened and Flumpkin immediately switched off the torch again.

"Are they really witches?" Emma whispered to me.

I nodded.

"Let's just get out of here as quick as we can," I said once I'd caught my breath. We headed for the exit to Creevely's office and saw the light filtering beneath the worn out door. Peeping through the keyhole, I could see her in conversation with the Gaye Wood elves but didn't get a chance to listen because a moment later, we heard heavy footfalls coming down the corridor.

"Can we hide?" I asked in a whisper.

"I doubt we'll fool them a second time," Clutterbutt replied. "It's better that we make as much distance between them and us as possible now."

We turned and ran. Where we were going, I didn't know. Once again, I felt the darkness close in on me, trying to suck the air out of my lungs. And then, turning a corner, we came across a wooden door similar to the one we'd entered through earlier. In an instant, Flumpkin had it open and we cascaded out of the ancient corridor into the welcoming embrace of the cold night air. I breathed in huge lung fulls, then realising we were still in danger, desperately looked around to get our bearings.

"We're in the car park!" whispered Emma.

"Let's get back in the car," I whispered urgently to Flumpkin.

"No probs," he replied, pulling the keys out of his pocket. Then, suddenly, the colour drained from his face.

"I can't remember where I parked it," he whispered, large tears appearing in his eyes.

"You're joking!"

"I can't!"

There was nothing for it.

"Run for it!!" I shouted.

We all ran helter skelter for the school gate. A loud bang behind us resonated throughout the school grounds and I imagined the witches had probably dispelled with the niceties of stopping at closed doors.

On and on we ran, and none of us stopped until we reached Emma's house. I collapsed in a heap by her front gate and Clutterbutt flopped down by the lawn, demolishing a whole flower bed in the process.

"How on earth are we going to get my dad's car back?" I asked in between heaving gulps of air.

"It's OK, the spell will have worn off by tomorrow morning," Clutterbutt panted. "We can sneak in first thing and steal it back and no-one will be any the wiser. I'm just glad I changed the number plates now because no-one's going to be able to trace the car back to you – by the way," he added. "Have either of you noticed the sky at all?"

I looked up and my jaw nearly hit the floor. Whilst the navy-blue night sky was mostly clear, there were still a few clouds dotted here and there. Of these, a few of the smaller ones had a strange iridescent orange glow about their edges as if illuminated by some giant astral street lamp.

"What is it?" I asked.

"I don't know," Flumpkin replied, averting his gaze. "One thing I do know, though, we're going to have to alert the Lord Lieutenant back in Northern Fairyland – one witch is bad enough but two together…"

"How are we going to do that?" I asked. "If you haven't noticed we still don't have that ethereal key."

Flumpkin thought for a minute.

"You said that you and Clutterbutt saw the two witches emerge from beneath that old stage?"

"That's right."

"That's probably where their coven is located. It might well be they've found the Ethereal Key for themselves and are using it to get other witches out of Northern Fairyland. I think tomorrow we're going to have to try and get into their coven and carry on searching."

"You've got to be kidding," moaned Clutterbutt.

"With a bit of luck we should be able to find the Key quite quickly," said Flumpkin, although I could see in the pale light his face had drained of all its colour. "That way," he went on, "We should be able to get back to Queen Mab's before you can say, 'wings and biscuits,' and once we've alerted the Lord Lieutenant, why, we'll be heroes! They might even make us knight protectors! Just think, Clutterbutt, your own suit of golden armour, your own winged steed..."

"Right now, I'd just settle for kitchen boy," moaned Clutterbutt.

Tears welled up in his eyes and I couldn't help feeling sorry for him. Most people had phobias; I'd been stung by a wasp on my lip as a baby and could no longer tolerate them buzzing around me without performing more karate moves than a Ken Lee movie. Wasn't sure I'd ever come across someone with 'witchophobia' before though.

"I'll do it," I said, making my mind up in an instant. "I'll go down into the coven with you, Flumpkin. Let's face it, we're going to need somebody to get my dad's car back home and Clutterbutt could do that with Emma."

Next instant I was squashed in a vice-like grip as Clutterbutt gave me the biggest hug a fairy could ever give a teenager.

"You're so brave, Guy," he said sobbing.

I looked at Emma. Her eyes shone like diamonds in a sun-kissed, rainbow glade.

"Be careful, tomorrow, Guy," she mouthed.

CHAPTER TEN – The Underground City

Though I was still concerned about my father's Mercedes, the next day began quite well. Emma had already been quite busy when we called for her.

"I spoke to Will on the phone last night when I got back in," she told us whilst putting on her favourite baseball jacket. "He's found details for about six circuses around Manchester, and he's getting a bus rover ticket this morning with Di even as we speak – they're going to visit each one and try and find Mr Mystico for us."

It was only eight-o-clock when we arrived at the school and must have looked a strange sight going through the front gate: Me in my blazer; Flumpkin in fishnets and skirt; Cluterbutt in his red leather jacket; and Emma looking pleased as punch with her arm through mine.

Our smiles quickly disappeared when we walked into the car-parking compound though. The two Gaye Wood elves were standing with Miss Antonio; she was talking and gesticulating wildly at something on the back of a recovery truck. My heart sank when I saw the silvery grey of my father's Mercedes then promptly did a double somersault when I noticed a massive great big dent on the driver's door.

Once again, a vision of Tremerwick Towers formed in my mind's eye. I felt my cheeks burning hot, followed swiftly by my neck and ears. Slowly I turned to face Flumpkin, who swallowed hard.

"It can still be fixed," he muttered.

As if to make matters worse, the engine on the recovery truck roared into life. It moved off and we had to stand aside to let it past. Fortunately, we got the phone number and company logo on the door.

"Come on," said Emma to Clutterbutt. "You and me might as well get after that truck and get Guy's dad's car back." She turned to me and with a squeeze of my arm, added, "Don't worry, I've got a plan – we'll see you round about dinner time."

At that, she took off, dragging a protesting Clutterbutt with her.

Flumpkin and I were both curious and we walked over towards where the elves and the Biology teacher were talking. On the way, I couldn't help but notice two very puzzled-looking council workmen busily repairing two badly charred doors on the main school building.

"What happened?" I asked them in as innocent a voice I could muster.

"You'd better ask those two idiot cops," said the first workman. "Here all night on special watch duty and didn't see a thing, the pair of wusses. I reckon some kids must've gotten loose with a flame thrower or a bazooka or something – in my day it was 'knock door run'. Makes you wonder whatever the world's comin' too, it does."

We headed over towards the elves. Even at the distance I could hear Miss Antonio complaining nineteen to the dozen.

"I'm – a tellin' you," she said in her strong Italian accent. "I was driving into da carpark just ten minutes ago. Then I heard a bang but I saw-a nothing. I went to da phone to phone da cops, came back and still saw-a nothing; then I went to tell Mrs Creevely and came back and found da two of you looking at-a my car and the huge silver car which had appeared out of nowhere. But I'm – a tellin' you, da silver car wasn't there when I crashed."

"Perhaps," said the first elf, tearing another page off his notebook and throwing it onto the floor beneath him to join a half dozen similar pages. "You only thought you didn't see the silver Mercedes. Perhaps it was such a terrible shock you didn't notice it, especially with it being so silvery and first thing in the misty morning fog…"

At that, Miss Antonio threw her arms in the air, uttered a dreadful tirade of Italian swear words and stormed off.

"Ooooh! She is a feisty one, isn't she?" said the second elf. He turned around, noticed me and Flumpkin and added, "You two shouldn't be here, this is official police business."

"Hold on," said the second elf, taking off his sunglasses to reveal his grey eyes. "It's Guy Foulkstone isn't it? And who's this – ah – delightful young lady you've got with you."

Both the elves were now eyeing Flumpkin with interest, and I began to wonder if it had been such a good idea to come over and talk.

"Britney Blenkinstrop," said Flumpkin suddenly, with an annoying flutter of his false eyelashes. "I'm an exchange student from New York. Guy Foulkstone here is kindly showing me around the school a bit before lessons and I must say, I simply lurve the uniforms you British policemen wear."

"They are rather fetching, aren't they?" said the second elf doing a twirl like a model on a fashion catwalk and sticking his arm up in a rather peculiar way. This immediately brought some very unsavoury words from the direction of the two workmen.

"So, what happened here?" I asked as innocently as possible. "Has it got anything to do with those two escaped lunatics you told us about?"

"I doubt it," said the first elf with a yawn. "The two of us were here last night at Mrs Creevely's request. I think she was afraid the two lunatics would try breaking into the school, though what for I don't know – as for this incident," he added, gesticulating to Mrs Antonio's car. "We've no idea where the Mercedes came from; K-one-five-five, M-one, A-five-five is not a recognised British registration mark so we don't know who the owner is." "It's on its way to the police pound even as we speak," said the second elf.

We left the Gaye wood elves and a sudden idea struck me.

"Flumpkin," I whispered. "It's Thursday morning and we've got football – not everyone usually turns up for registration first thing as it gets done after everyone's showered. If you want, you could put us under your invisibility charm and we could sneak past those workmen and get into the passage. I reckon the witches will be keeping a low profile now with the two workmen about so this might be our best chance."

A big grin spread across Flumpkin's face.

"Let's do it," he said.

A few minutes later, we were standing in the old assembly hall where I'd first seen the witches emerging from the stage. We both had torches and shone them around; but there was nothing to suggest anything untoward had happened the previous night. The hazy black cloud had disappeared, too. A small wooden podium stood in its place.

"Hold on a second," said Flumpkin, producing his wand. He mumbled a few words and gave it a swish, then added, "Watch this!"

The podium evaporated, and the shiny black cloud reappeared in its place whirling and broiling angrily like a cauldron full of snakes. Beneath it, the handle and unmistakable outline of a trapdoor appeared. I felt an icy stab of fear run down my back and shivered involuntarily. And then came the familiar gnawing at my stomach and tinkling sound in my ears.

"You can feel it, too, can't you," said Flumpkin, studying me with interest. "It looks to me like they've cast a camouflage spell."

Without even a second thought, he pulled open the trapdoor and clambered in. I followed and felt the unyielding uneven texture of well-worn stone beneath my feet. Shining my torch around me, I realised I was standing on the top of a narrow spiralling stone staircase held within curving, roughly-hewn stone walls. It reminded me of my 'unscheduled holiday' in Wales some years back after running away from Tremerwick Towers. I'd visited a castle there and gone up and down similar winding steps in a tall narrow tower.

As silently and as quickly as possible, we descended the stone spiral staircase. The further down we went, the lighter it seemed to get, although I use the term 'light' in its loosest possible sense. It was more of a rather uncomfortable pulsating dull green glow to be honest emanating through narrow arrow slits in the wall.

After a few minutes of this, I unexpectedly bumped into Flumpkin. He did not complain, however; instead he shushed his finger to his lip and pointed below at an arched ancient wooden door. Pulsating dull green light shone through gaps between its shrunken shrivelled timbers illuminating thick shiny studded metal bolts on the surface. For a moment, I felt we were about to enter the heart chamber of an enormous slavering beast.

Cautiously, Flumpkin tried the heavy wrought iron handle. The door was unlocked. Slowly but surely we pushed it open. At the last few inches it creaked horribly and we both cringed.

Nothing happened and Flumpkin stepped out first. He let out a mighty gasp and when I followed I saw why.

Before us lay a cobbled street, enclosed either side by large circular-windowed, bee-hive shaped dwellings which easily stood up to three storeys high. In the green-glowing gloomy distance, we saw several circular stone towers looming higher, disappearing up into the dimly-lit darkness like colossal pillars holding back a solid sky. The pulsating, green glow cast weird shadows on the walls and up the dark alleyways. They resembled long-forgotten wraiths and indeed, the whole town seemed deserted as if it hadn't seen anything living in centuries.

Closer inspection of the nearest beehive-shaped dwelling revealed glass windows frosted with age; smooth earth-brown walls not too dissimilar to glazed earthenware pottery; and a shrivelled wooden front door with runic figures.

"It's Ancient Elfish writing," whispered Flumpkin, tracing the contours with his wand tip. "I'd translate it too only it's a Level Five spell and would probably give us away. You can bet your last fairy farthing those Gaye Wood elves upstairs know about this place, too, and are letting the witches use it."

"But for what reason?" I asked.

"I don't know but if we look for the source of this light we might find something. It might be dragon plasma which means it came from Northern Fairyland."

We continued on our way and although we were still under Flumpkin's invisibility charm my neck prickled as though we were being watched. In the distance, the pulsating green light was at its brightest; like some eerie sunset on an alien world.

"What do you think happened here?" I asked as we headed towards it.

"I don't really know," Flumpking replied. "Fairies and elves never did see eye to eye. I think the elves were jealous of our magic and human magic also."

"Humans are magic, too?"

Flumpkin laughed.

"Humans are probably the most magical creatures in the universe and probably the stupidest, too. I mean, who in their right mind could write music and books and plays and poetry the way you humans do then go along and say there is no such thing as magic?"

"But it's not magic," I persisted.

"Isn't it? Why, some of the most powerful spells I've ever heard of are written ones – there's one called a Shadowscript

– it's so powerful, you can use it to control somebody's entire life."

I thought for a minute at what Flumpkin had told me. Then something struck me: "You said the elves were jealous of fairy magic and human magic," I whispered. "Did that mean fairies, elves and humans lived together?"

"They did, once upon a time," Flumpkin replied. "But that was about four thousand years ago and only in Britain. In those days, this country was held in high esteem throughout the world. Our craftsmen were the finest and our trading vessels went to every port and every corner of the globe. Then the elves discovered science and started to use rational explanations for everything. Anything they couldn't explain they called 'evil sorcery' and waged a terrible war on humans and fairies alike throughout Britain. In the end, most humans renounced magic and joined with the elves. Us poor fairies had to make ourselves another world which we did by forging the Ethereal Key and crossing over to it.

"The rest you know from your history books. The elves made such a mess of things; Britain was reduced to being a land of warring tribes and wound up getting invaded by the Romans."

It was an interesting alternative history lesson but doubtful I'd see it on the History syllabus anytime soon! I was about to ask another question when we turned a corner into what looked like a main square and came across the source of the green light. There it was, a swirling, whirling, pulsating mini green sun encaged in a megalithic stone circle that for all the world resembled a smaller version of Stonehenge. Something else was held within the circle, too, like black globules piled up in stacks. It was only when we got closer I realised what they were: piles upon piles of black bin bags filled to bursting with books; just like what Will and I had seen that time back in the library some months back.

"Definitely dragon plasma," whispered Flumpkin.

CHAPTER ELEVEN – The Pumpkin Garden

"Don't touch it," said Flumpkin as I reached out to the nearest standing stone. He reached into his school bag and pulled out an apple I'd given him earlier then threw it at the stone circle. There was a sudden flash and it fell at my feet, smouldering.

"Instant apple sauce," said Flumpkin with a sardonic grin. "Now *that's* magic!"

We walked around the stone circle perimeter and I noticed one of the rubbish bags had burst open and spilled its contents to reveal several Vexatious Vlad the Volgograd Vampyre stories and a bundle of books with the characteristic Jenny Fiton signature. There were even a few Flumpkin and Clutterbutt novels which amused Flumpkin no end.

Why on earth had all these books been brought here I wondered - especially as they were supposed to have been shredded.

"Come on," said Flumpkin with a grin. "Let's see if we can find anything in this underground town to get into that circle. I'm sure the Ethereal Key is held inside that green sun."

"What are we looking for?" I asked.

"I'm guessing, I think we'll be needing mistletoe berries or something like that to break the stone barrier."

Biology wasn't my strongest subject but even I knew that plants needed sunlight and didn't grow underground. Something also told me mistletoe berries were only available in the winter – at least, I always associated them with Christmas-time. I started thinking of Emma, too; and the flowery-smelling perfume she liked to wear from time to time.

"This way I think," said Flumpkin suddenly.

We continued down one of the cobbled streets leading off the square. I noticed it seemed to get warmer the further we walked, and the shadows became less and less due to a barely discernible cubic-shaped sun glowering through the haze above us. It could have almost been a balmy summer day but for the strange alien surroundings.

After a few minutes, we came across a tall grey stone wall with an arched entrance sealed by an ancient wooden doorway. Flumpkin tried the shiny metal knob but found it wouldn't open. He immediately repeated his invisible key trick and the lock yielded with a satisfying click.

"Bound to be some mistletoe in here," he said in a low voice.

It was then I noticed a sign written in old-fashioned English.

Magyck Garden most foul

Do not feed the plants

"Is it safe?" I whispered, remembering the previous day's escapade with the plant in Biology.

"Why shouldn't it be?" grinned Flumpkin pushing open the door.

His grin suddenly disappeared and the colour drained from his face.

"Wings and biscuits," he uttered.

Over his shoulder I saw row upon row of what looked like armchair-sized pumpkins. They had the same orange-brown colouration and would easily have passed off as such were it not for the fact that they wobbled on their mossy-green beds; uttered strange hissing sounds; and were attached from their tops by green fronds to thick large leafy stems.

"Rock goblins," whispered Flumpkin, slowly closing the door again. "This is worse than I thought."

"You mean those plants were goblins?" I retorted.

"The worst kind – growing them is actually banned in Northern Fairyland. Witches tend to use them as soldiers and servants because it's not in a rock goblin's nature to ask questions – but to grow so many – there must be at least a thousand in there."

"Would weedkiller help?" I asked, remembering our gardener kept a large container in one of our back sheds.

"What's weedkiller?"

I explained and Flumpkin's upper lip curled in disgust.

"You can't go round killing babies," he hissed. "Even if they are rock goblins – no, they'll have to go back to Northern Fairyland – at least there they can go into a park along with the witches we saw."

"We still need to get into that stone circle though and we still need berries; how are we going to get past them?" I asked.

Frumpin grinned.

"Don't forget, we're still invisible."

Cautiously, we opened the door and stole past the rows of goblin pumpkins. Something tickled my nose and for one dreadful moment I had the urge to sneeze. Fortunately, I managed to suppress it.

"This'll do," whispered Flumpkin stopping at what looked like a clump of mistletoe growing around the trunk of an apple tree.

"There's no berries," I whispered.

"Watch!"

He pulled his wand out and gave a low utterance followed by a series of swishes. The transformation was almost instantaneous and a rich crop of white berries appeared.

"Simple Level Two maturation spell," he whispered.

A sudden series of popping noises behind us followed by a strange chittering and chattering noise made me look over my shoulder. Flumpkin froze in fear. The nearest pumpkins were moving more vigourously now.

"Wings and biscuits," he hissed. "I think my spell's affected the rock goblins, too."

The chittering noise grew louder. We hurriedly gathered some berries and made our way back along the path we'd taken. All around us the orange pumpkins were now breaking open. Like chickens coming out of eggs, the chittering chattering rock goblins were emerging; stretching as if waking from a long sleep and yawning to reveal mouthfuls of needle-sharp teeth. They all looked the same, too: knee-height, large black malevolent eyes, thick black beards, bald heads and thick muscular arms.

To my enormous relief, the entrance to the garden loomed before us and we quickened our pace. Then, to my horror, I felt my nose got itchy again and realised the cause was a nearby lavender bush. Something about lavender always made me sneeze.

"a-a-a…"

Placing a shaking hand to my nose, I pinched it and tried to hold my breath. Relief.

"Hurry, Flumpkin," I hissed.

We reached the door and then the overwhelming urge to sneeze came again.

"a-a-a…"

Flumpkin went white.

"Don't," he hissed. "You'll break the rest of the invisibility spell."

I pinched my nose again.

He turned the knob.

The urge to sneeze returned again and this time I couldn't hold it back.

"ACHOO!"

The garden fell silent. I turned to look behind and my blood ran cold. A thousand pairs of eyes stared daggers. Slowly, the now massed ranks of rock goblins edged towards us.

"Run!" shouted Flumpkin. He then held up his wand and shouted, "Reveal footsteps!"

All at once, two glowing pairs of footprints appeared on the cobbled path outside. Without a second thought, we took off, following them in the direction away from the roiling riot of rock goblins.

A long low ululating call filled the air and a few seconds later, it was replaced by the sound of a thousand tiny footsteps echoing on the cobblestones. As I ran, I wondered if Flumpkin still felt hostile to my original weed killer idea. It was too late now though. And what would happen if they caught us?

"When we get back to the entrance tower," Flumpkin panted. "I'll use a Level Eight sealing spell on the door; that should hold them back!"

"Won't it alert the elves, too?" I shouted.

"We'll worry about them afterwards!"

The entrance tower loomed ahead of us in the distance; its gloomy appearance strangely welcoming. I focussed on the ancient wooden door. Closer and closer it got. Suddenly, Flumpkin screamed and fell head over heals, his fishnet stockings ripping on the cobblestones.

"My ankle," he moaned, rocking to and fro and cradling it. "I've jarred my ankle!"

For a second, I was tempted to keep running but there was no way I could leave him to the rock goblins. Goodness knows what they would've done to him. And talking about rock goblins, I could see their boiling mass of heads, arms and legs rapidly approaching us.

"Flumpkin," I shouted, grabbing his arm. "Get up, they'll be on us in a few seconds."

"I can't," he whimpered.

My already jack-hammering heart now felt as though it would burst out of my chest. Desperately, I looked around. There was no way we could make it to the tower in time. Flumpkin was too big and heavy-looking for me to carry.

"My wand," Flumpkin gasped, tears in his eyes and pointing.

A few yards from him was his wand; its tip glowing slightly. Without a second thought I ran over. My fingers wrapped around the thin wood. A tingling sensation began at my hands, up my arms and through my whole body as though electricity was coursing through my veins and sinews. Stronger and stronger the feeling grew and time almost slowed to a standstill.

"Back!" I shouted, spinning round and pointing the wand at the onrushing horde.

There was a dull thudding sound and the oncoming roiling mass slowed dramatically. It was as though an invisible, shimmering glass wall had sprung up in front of them. The momentum of the goblin charge brought the magical barrier closer until it slowed to a halt within a few yards of us. With wide-eyed looks, the ugly little creatures piled up in front of it a good ten bodies high; some that could were waving their little fists at us, others had their mouths right up against the barrier and resembled large sucker fish in a tank.

The wide-eyed look on Flumpkin's face was almost comical to behold.

I handed the wand back to Flumpkin and he ran it over his sprained ankle, muttering a few more barely audible words.

"That's what I meant you to do," he added, getting up and testing his leg. "Still, no harm done, come on, let's get back up to the school."

He turned round and made a very rude gesture at the immobilised goblins then we made our way to the entrance tower. Once inside, Flumpkin made a few incantations to seal the door.

"What are we going to do about the Ethereal Key?" I asked him as he put his wand away.

"Have you got a chemistry lab in this school?" Flumpkin replied.

"Yes."

"Good, I'm sure they'll have some camphor there. It's a really good goblin repellent. That way, we can go back down and finish up the job."

We hurried up the stairs, taking them three at a time and got out through the trap door. We stood on the stage and surveyed it for a few seconds.

"I suppose we'd better return it to its original state," Flumpkin muttered, pulling out his wand.

"That'll hardly be necessary, dearie," cackled a high-pitched voice.

Suddenly, out of the shadows loomed a tall figure with a long scraggy cloak. For a brief second I didn't recognise the voice, then it occurred to me who it was.

"You," I said.

"Indeed," cackled Mrs Creevely's secretary, holding up a twisted sliver of wood that crackled and hissed in the thick musty air.

Several other figures materialised in the darkness. Some with pointed hats, others with cloaks fluttering in the now icy draft. Each carried a twisted sliver of wood.

"Back," shouted Flumpkin, holding his wand up.

His command was met by a kaleidoscopic flash of green, orange, yellow and electric blue light. Unseen hands gripped the inside of my stomach from behind, yanked me back forcefully and the room span.

CHAPTER TWELVE – The Squirrel in the Dungeon

"I wondered when I'd see you, Guy."

An old nineteen-thirties newsreel was playing in my head and a thousand black and white German soldiers were goose-stepping on my brain. The inside of my mouth felt like the Sahara Desert complete with dead furry animals and my fingers tingled with pins and needles.

"Over here!"

The floor was cold and hard beneath me save a thin smattering of prickly straw, and the place itself was dark as though I'd woken just before the break of dawn. Fumbling around, I could feel another besides me, breathing rhythmically yet unstirred.

"Your girlfriend is still asleep," said the voice, a man's voice and one that was yet curiously familiar. A picture came into my head of the man: tall, black combed-back hair, droopy black moustache and a permanent grin. A writer who once came to our school.

"Mr Mystico?" I said, but I'm sure it just came out as a mumble.

"None other!"

There was a click of a cigarette lighter and a large candle was lit. Slowly, the room came into focus. Flumpkin was indeed fast asleep but the sight of Mr Mystico made me recoil in horror.

No longer combed back, his hair looked unkempt as though he'd been dragged through a hedge backwards then body-slammed by a hippo for good measure. He had a shaggy beard, too; and his eyes were wide like saucers, though whether it was from the shock of seeing me or something else, I couldn't tell.

"Christ, you look like Rasputin!" I said, rubbing my head. "Where on earth are we?"

"A dungeon, we're in a dungeon in Grendlewick to be precise."

"Where on earth is Grendlewick?"

"An ancient Elfish town. I didn't even know it existed until the witches brought me here over a week ago. You can imagine my surprise when I found out it was directly beneath your school."

"You know about the witches, too, then?" I asked.

Mr Mystico nodded, and I proceeded to tell him all about the strange events I'd witnessed over the last few days, starting with the herd of wildebeest. Curiously enough, he didn't seem surprised when I mentioned the appearance of Flumpkin and Clutterbutt; he just nodded his head as though characters from story books came to life every day of the week.

"So this girl with you is actually Flumpkin in disguise," Mr Mystico concluded once I'd told him about our capture by the witches. "My word, that is interesting. You know, all this would make an absolutely splendid novel if we ever get out of this alive. I can see it now – The Clutterbutt and Flumpkin Caper. Me, signing copies for thousands of wide-eyed children at every large book store in the country…"

"What are these witches going to do with us?" I asked. The words I'd heard one utter about a 'red river of wine' and 'entombed in a book' and 'Gatekeeper' were reverberating in my mind.

"Oh, I thought that bit was obvious," Mr Mystico replied. "My knowledge of witchcraft is not brilliant but I suspect they're going to use us as a Midsummer sacrifice. Those books you saw at the standing stones, I think they intend to bring them all to life and unleash them as an army. At least that's what I heard them say and I've seen them do enough magic to believe them, too."

"But these things don't happen in real life," I persisted. "You can't bring characters to life out of books."

"My dear Guy, I always thought you at least had a proper imagination. By your own admission, you have lived with two such characters over the last few days. Just as I, too, have – ah – suffered."

There was a sudden grunt and two glowing eyes appeared in a dark corner.

"If he disses me one more time," said a squeaky voice. "I'll shove my paintbrushes so far up his sorry ass, he'll be talking in Technicolor for the rest of his miserable life!"

"See what I mean," said Mr Mystico. "That has to be the worst American accent this side of a spaghetti western."

"I wouldn't be too sure of that," I whispered, looking over at the still sleeping Flumpkin.

The owner of the voice emerged from the shadows and for the second time in the dungeon I recoiled: more in surprise than in horror though. A grey squirrel stood before us; an unnaturally large one, too. A good two and a half feet tall, its arms were slightly longer in proportion to what you'd expect in a normal squirrel. It held several paintbrushes in its paws and had a large bushy tail streaked with blue, green and orange paints.

"What's wrong with you Limeys?" it squeaked, the tip of its tail glowing slightly. "Anyone would think you'd never seen a squirrel before!"

"I've already told you," snapped Mr Mystico. "You are not a proper squirrel; you are an animalivra. A book that's been brought to life using witchcraft." He turned to me, then added, "Same goes for your friend there; he's an animalivra, too."

"You're joking!"

For some reason, I felt a sinking in my heart. To have Flumpkin and Clutterbutt's existences explained in such black and white terms seemed to give them less substance, less of an anchor in reality. To be honest, I'd started to believe their story about coming from Northern Fairyland. I'd even found myself wondering what it was like to live there, whether they had magical cities, dragons, pirates and knights in shining armour. Perhaps at the back of my mind there'd been a secret longing to go and visit the place when the two fairies crossed back over. All that had been dashed now, and I found myself hating Flumpkin and Clutterbutt for being such a pair of phoneys. It didn't occur to me that it wasn't their fault and they hadn't asked to be turned from books to fairies.

"I don't care what you stupid Limeys think," squeaked the squirrel suddenly. And I noticed the paintbrushes it held were glowing slightly from the tips in the flickering candle light. "You can deny my existence if you like," it went on, "and you can deny that sleeping fairy's existence for all I care; but what you can't do is: deny the existence of artistic genius."

With the tips of his tail and paintbrushes glowing even brighter, he picked up the candle and used it to illuminate the dungeon walls. I noticed several paintings of trees and acorns and something suddenly clicked as though a lightbulb had been turned on inside my befuddled state.

"You're Splooshy, aren't you?" I said.

"Well whaddya know," squeaked the squirrel in triumph. "Recognition at last; I had to work my butt off for these pictures, you know. It's not easy being this talented!"

"You painted the town hall and a police station, too?" I suggested.

"Yup! All my own work. I'd just started to paint on this beautifully-sculpted metal tree when these, whaddya call 'em? Beaches? Blew it up and captured me."

That explained the destruction of the mobile phone mast. The council had actually made it look like a tree to blend in.

"But where did you come from?" I asked.

"Hell, I don't rightly recall. The first thing I ever saw was this green light and these tall stones and black bin bags full of books. Yesterday, when the beaches caught me, they said they was gonna take me back there on Midsummers day along with some other dudes and use us as a magi-catalyst-thingamabob."

"He means the sacrifice," interjected Mr Mystico. "I think they plan to sacrifice us at the Grendlewick stones and like I said, use it in some weird spell to bring all those books to life."

A thought occurred to me.

"The witch I heard mentioned something about a person called a 'last vessel' being necessary for the sacrifice; any idea what they meant?"

"You or Flumpkin, probably," Mr Mystico replied.

"Midsummer's tomorrow isn't it?" I said, feeling a wave of panic spread through my chest.

"Yes."

"Hadn't we better do something?"

"Don't you think I, sorry we, that is, the book and me, have already tried. I've worn my fingers to the bone trying to loosen these rocks – it's impossible."

"We could always use my wand," groaned a voice beside me. Flumpkin was starting to stir.

"Stupid creature," said Mr Mystico. "These are real witches. Do you honestly think they'd leave you with a wand in this dungeon!"

Flumpkin sat up suddenly and his eyes narrowed.

"Don't call me a creature!" he snapped rubbing his head. "I'm a fairy and up until a few years back I was a page in the court of Queen Mabiley. You might like skulking around in dungeons looking like you came off second best in a tussle with a dung troll but at least I take pride in my appearance."

He gave a flick of his hair and a loud sniffle.

"He's got a point you know," said Splooshy. "Even if he is dressed like a broad. Just because you're made from paper and ink it doesn't mean you ain't got feelings, too."

Even in the candle light, I could see the colour change in Flumpkin's face. First red, then purple.

"For the last time," he yelled. "I'm not some figment of your imaginations; I'm not made from paper and ink like some witch's book demon. I'M A REAL FAIRY!"

He broke into loud sobs. Not the sort of superficial ones you get when a child grazes his knee but deep guttural ones that sounded as though each corner of his heart and soul had been doused in slug repellent and tied to the back end of a giant snail.

I'm not the sort to give boys hugs, especially boys dressed as girls, but in this case, I made an exception and held him close.

"Do you think I enjoy being stuck in this world?" he went on in between gulps. "Three whole years I've been here! Have you ever stopped to wonder if I miss my mother and father who are probably worried sick about me; my sister Bianca and her beautiful flower jewels; the rides through the White Mountains on my Uncle Marcus's skyboat? I even miss him calling me 'Stinkerbell' all the time."

Mr Mystico flashed a quick glance in my direction and his mouth dropped wide open.

"But none of that is in my novels," he said incredulously. "Sure, I put those details into my notes but I never used them. Even Guy mentioned the name 'Stinkerbell' once. Tell me, what is your sister's favourite pet?"

"Snowdrop the Unicorn."

"And her favourite flower jewel?"

"The ruby bluebells."

Mr Mystico's eyes grew wider. Slowly he turned to Splooshy.

"Splooshy," he said in a gentle voice. "What is your sister's name?"

"How the hell should I know?" Splooshy retorted. His manner suddenly changed though and his face became warmer. "Thanks for calling me by my proper name," he added.

"Now that is curious," said Mr Mystico, rubbing his unkempt beard. "In my notes but not in the novel I had you down as having two sisters: Jemima and Beatrix. Yet here, unlike Flumpkin, you have no knowledge. So why the difference?"

Something clicked inside my head.

"The Gaye Wood elves, they told me they'd been after Flumpkin and Clutterbutt for the last few years but the books were only taken a month or so ago."

"Most curious," said Mr Mystico.

There was a sudden blinding flash and a sound of splintering wood. Almost as if on cue, two policemen in motorcycle helmets stood in the remains of the doorway to the dungeon cell.

"If you value your lives, you'd better come with us!" said the first Gaye wood elf.

CHAPTER THIRTEEN – The Battle of Creevely's Office

I was loathed to trust the two elves. However, Mr Mystico and Splooshy had no qualms whatsoever and were up in a flash. Even Flumpkin got up and moved hesitatingly towards them across the dimly lit straw-covered stone floor.

"Are you coming or what?" said the second elf, looking at me in disgust. "This camphor we're wearing is not going to hold off those rock goblins forever, you know! Gordon Bennet!" he added. "The things we do for you people. We're going to have to shower in Beau Parfum de fleurs aftershave for at least a month to get rid of this smell."

"You do reek a bit," squeaked Splooshy, his whiskers twitching.

Still unsure, I got up, too, and moved slowly towards the remains of the dungeon door.

"Come on. Hurry!"

Everyone moved off at a steady jog. Not wanting to be left alone, I followed in their wake. We ran up a narrow passage lined with similar heavy dungeon doors. It led us into a large torch lit hall. Where we were going I didn't have a clue. Still jogging, the elves led us up several flights of well-worn steps - our footfalls echoing against the high stone walls. It must have been some sight: two motorcycle cops; a large squirrel carrying paintbrushes with glowing tips; a bearded man in what looked like a ring masters outfit; a boy fairy dressed as a girl; and me, running behind them, shaking my head in disbelief.

In the flickering light of the flaming torches, I noticed small groups of bald-headed rock goblins skulking in the shadows. Some of them were wafting their hands vigorously in front of their faces and eyeing us as though we were something they'd fond stuck to the bottom of their bare feet.

Shortly, we reached the main square of Grendlewick. The eerie green light and smooth light tan pottery-like walls of the buildings seemed to scream at us to get out fast. I wondered whether to ask about the Ethereal key. However, just at that moment, one of the more adventurous goblins, whilst holding its nose tried to grab at the first elf. It failed dismally and ended up doing a double somersault. It then ran off in the direction of an ancient-looking dried-out fountain, squealing in a high pitched tone.

It didn't take long after that to get to the tower and back into the old school building through the stage trapdoor. Fortunately there was no sign of any witches.

"This should keep the goblins at bay," said the second elf, throwing a bottle of camphor back down the stairs. The echo of the breaking glass seemed to go on forever. He slammed the trapdoor shut and between us, we manhandled one of the rusting pieces of machinery from the old woodwork room into the old hall and onto the stage. As we moved it into place to weigh the trapdoor down I glanced at my watch. Four-thirty! We'd only been down there seven or eight hours. It felt like it had been a lot longer. I wondered where Emma was; and Will, Di and Clutterbutt, too. Had they reported us missing?

"How did you know we were down there?" panted Flumpkin as though reading my mind.

"You kidding," said the second elf with a grin. "The size of that blocking spell you did earlier; it must have registered on every Hexometer within a hundred-mile radius.

"What blocking spell?" I retorted.

"The one you did, Guy," whispered Flumpkin. "It was a Level twenty! Even in Northern Fairyland that's quite an achievement!"

I felt my cheeks flush warm.

"We've been watching this area for some time now," said the second elf. "What with all the witches that seem to be coming and going – come on," he added, making a final check that the trapdoor was secure. "We'd better go and see the boss. If I'm not mistaken, we're in for a long night."

"Who on earth is the boss?" I asked, starting to feel very confused.

"You'll see."

The two elves led us into the corridor. We followed them past the walls with their cracked plaster and mouldering paintwork down to a door set in the wall. I immediately recognised it as the first elf turned the handle - Mrs Creevely's office!

"She's not?" I whispered.

"Mrs Creevely's the area commander for Elf Intelligence," whispered the second elf as we all trooped in. It was funny. I'd been in the room so many times before though not from this particular angle because we were right behind Mrs Creevely's high-backed leather chair and leather-topped table.

"Good afternoon," said Mrs Creevely swivelling her chair round to face us. "Goodness Gracious! What on earth are you?" she exclaimed on seeing Splooshy. Her eyes then fell on me, Flumpkin and Mr Mystico in quick succession. "I see you've no doubt met some of the local witches, too, by the looks of you," she went on. "Hmm, I think you could all do with a nice cup of tea – with a stiff shot of brandy, too – by the looks of you."

She picked up her phone and pushed a few numbers. I was getting more and more confused by the minute. It was so unlike her to be nice. Suddenly, something inside me clutched at my stomach and I'm sure my heart must have stopped for a brief second. I knew exactly who was on the other end of the phone.

"Don't," I hissed.

But it was too late.

"Yes, Miss Macbeth; we've found Guy and Britney, inform Guy's housekeeper – yes, yes, they look as though they've been through a terrible ordeal, even got some sort of a rodent with them…"

Splooshy's grey cheeks flushed red.

"You fools…" cackled the voice on the other end; it was so loud, we could hear it echoing up the corridor and through the closed door of the Headmistress's office, too.

Mrs Creevely went white.

"She's one of them!" I shouted.

"He's right," shouted Flumpkin. He pointed to the filing cabinet by the door and said to the two elves, "Quick, help me get that over the door – it'll buy us all a few moments to escape!"

The next few moments happened as though someone had crushed a wasps nest inside a room full of headless chickens. Everyone seemed to be bumping into one another and getting in each others way. Like watching an action replay in slow motion, I saw the two elves with their shoulders against the door; Mrs Creevely reaching into her drawer; Flumpkin hiding underneath her table; and Splooshy trying to push past me, holding his brushes in the air.

Bang!

The room filled with smoke. An odour of sulphur permeated the air and my ears felt as though a troop of bell ringers were at work. Slowly, the smoke subsided to reveal: Splooshy, frozen with fear, his arms around my waist but still clutching his paintbrushes; the elves groaning on the floor; and Mrs Creevly pointing a revolver at the shape of Miss Macbeth in the doorway – the door itself hung by a single hinge and fell to the door with a crash.

"Do you honestly think that pathetic gun will stop me," cackled Miss Macbeth in a voice rank with derision. She held up a twisted wooden wand and a cold stab of fear ran down my spine.

"As a matter of fact, I do," replied Mrs Creevly, her voice calm and cold. "Now put that wand down and surrender yourself. You know full well that witchcraft is illegal in this country."

"It won't be much longer. Thanks to your two pathetic wizards, my sisters and I are going to take this whole city for ourselves."

Mrs Creevely's eyes fell on the two elves.

"Not those two fools, them," said Mrs Macbeth pointing her wand at me then Mr Mystico in turn.

Us? Wizards? What did she mean? Then it occurred to me both our grandfathers had been stage magicians. I'd not long cast a Level 20 spell. Was there a link somehow?

"Four years ago," Mrs Macbeth went on. "Those two foolish wizards wrote a shadowscript sealed in blood. They closed the gate between this world and Northern Fairyland. Very fortuitous really because Sister Narkarla happened to be on an unofficial visit to this world at the time."

"That closure of the link would explain the lack of contact we've had with Queen Mab these last few years," said Mrs Creevely, her voice still calm. "It doesn't explain the number of witches and spells we've been seeing lately, though. I'd say there's at least a dozen witches we've been keeping tabs on recently. If the link is shut, how come they're getting through it?"

Flumpkin, Mr Mystico and I looked at each other in disbelief. Mrs Creevely and her secretary were talking about Northern Fairyland as if it actually existed.

"Foolish elf!" spat Mrs Macbeth. "Sister Narkarla has spent these last four years recruiting her sisterhood from among the denizens of this world. I, too, was ignorant of my true power until I met her." She closed her eyes as though savouring a particularly pleasant meal then went on, "Slowly, Sister Narkarla has been imparting to us the ancient wisdom of our craft so true; fashioning us wands out of holly and yew; writing us books in blood, skin and sinew; showing us power that none of us knew; uniting us, Buddhist, Christian and Hindu ..."

As she spoke, I could feel the air start to crackle. Again, it was as if a rat was gnawing at my stomach. Mrs Creevely must have realised something was happening, too, because she immediately levelled her revolver and squeezed the trigger. There was a bang, a flash of blue light, followed by a zinging sound. A vase full of flowers on top of the filing cabinet exploded into a thousand pieces.

Mrs Macbeth gave another derisive laugh.

"My shield is too powerful for thee, and now for my spell, but what shall it be? I'll turn you into something, maybe. A worm? A slug? What about..."

Without thinking, I snatched one of Splooshy's glowing brushes and pointed it at Mrs Macbeth.

"I throw it back at thee!" I shouted in desperation.

A blinding flash of light filled every corner of the room. Mrs Macbeth disappeared and was replaced by a buzzing sound. A bee the size of a fist alighted on the leather-topped desk in front of Mrs Creevely who was looking at me with her mouth and eyes wide open.

"What did you do to me?" said the bee in a high-pitched buzz. "Turn me back at once! Turn me back at once or I'll sting every one of you!"

"Hardly a wise move," said Mrs Creevely with a laugh. She held out her hand and added, "go ahead, sting me if you like. And when you die afterwards like any other bee, I'll bury you in a shoe box."

"Please turn me back," pleaded the bee. "I'll do anything."

All eyes in the room turned on me.

"You'd better do it," whispered Flumpkin. "She'll die if she stays like that too long."

"If she does, it'll be her own fault," said Mrs Creevely, her voice now with its familiar coldness. "Dabbling in magic always comes with a price. That's why witchcraft is still illegal in this country. But go ahead, Guy, I'll make an exception in this case and let you turn her back "

Totally clueless, I gave one of the paintbrushes a wave.

"Turn her back," I said.

Nothing happened.

I waved the brush again.

"Er – waves of white and sea of blue, make this spell – er – undo?"

Still nothing happened.

The bee that was Mrs Macbeth let out a low moan.

"Please," she said. "I renounce my sisterhood and promise to serve you. Just turn me back."

"That's more like it," said Mr Mystico, suddenly. He stepped forward, took the brushes from me and gave them a little wave just above the bee.

"I pronounce you witch-free and untainted;

Your spell is broken and your bee unpainted!"

A substance like tiny glittery snowflakes fell from the tip of the brush and onto the bee. It promptly did several backflips, and a series of head spins that would have made Billy Beamish the Boston break-dance champion proud. Then before our very eyes, it grew larger and larger and as if in a bubbly cartoon mish-mash, slowly morphed back into Mrs Macbeth.

"How on earth did you know how to do that?" said Mrs Creevely, her eyes wide open.

Mr Mystico blew the edges of the paintbrushes as though he were blowing smoke from a gun.

"Simple," he said. "It was part of my last Flumpkin and Clutterbutt novel where they return to Northern Fairyland, the same one you had me banned from publishing – now," he added. "Mrs Macbeth, I really think you ought to tell us what you know. Because if I'm not mistaken, we're in a lot more trouble than any of us actually realise."

"I'll tell you whatever you want to know, but please, don't tell Narkarla – if she learns I have betrayed her, she will not rest until I am dead."

"I give you my word."

"And when I have my wand back, I will make everyone forget," added Flumpkin.

"Alas," said Mrs Macbeth. "The witches have your wand. You would be foolish to retrieve it for, there are another seventeen of them – together under Sister Narkarla we formed a Triple Hex."

Mrs Creevely had started attending to the two wounded elves but on hearing this, she gasped. Flumpkin shook his head and uttered something dreadful under his breath. Mr Mystico; however, looked unperturbed.

"Just as I thought," he said. "All the more reason for stopping them. Now, Mrs Macbeth, you mentioned earlier that I along with Guy here, produced a shadowscript. I'll be the first to admit my knowledge of witchcraft is not fantastic but even I know a shadowscript needs blood and is made invalid by burning it. Do you know exactly what the shadowscript was?"

"Yes, it was a sheet of paper with notes you made many years ago in a school, the one with blood stains on it."

The index finger on my left hand twinged; the exact same spot where a craft knife had slipped all those years ago when we first met Mr Mystico. I quickly reminded him.

"Yes," Mrs Macbeth went on. "A shadowscript is a dark contract and needs the blood of a powerful magician in order to seal it. That's why we've been watching you closely and the boy here. Yes, Mr Mystico, both you and Guy are, very, very powerful magicians.

"Sister Narkarla knew the way to Northern Fairyland had been sealed because she tried to return and failed. She also knew of the shadowscript because it emits a powerful aura; it is in her hands now, even as we speak."

Mr Mystico held up his hand to stop her.

"How did she obtain the shadowscript?" he asked. "All my notes were in a safe."

"With all due respect, Mr Mystico, we witches have our own ways of opening safes. I went to your flat with one of my Sisters last night and took the document." Mrs Macbeth paused for a second then added, "I'm sorry to say we also burned your flat down."

Mr Mystico let out a long breath and his face went purple. I could tell he was struggling to control himself. Funnily enough, I was sure I could see his thoughts, too. They seemed to involve him chasing a bee round Mrs Creevely's office with a can of insect spray.

"What of my laptop?" he asked. "Did they take that, too?"

"No, it must have been burned with all the other stuff."

Mr Mystico breathed heavily again.

"Actually, it's not," I said. "My friend Will has it. He took it from your house, yesterday. It's only a five-minute drive from here."

A look of relief washed over Mr Mystico's face.

"And your Sister Narkarla," he said, turning back to Mrs Macbeth. "She is preparing her own shadowscript? One that'll make her ruler of this city and ultimately this whole world?"

"How did you know that?"

"I wrote it as part of my last Clutterbutt and Flumpkin novel. I also know that once she starts and if she continues to follow my story plot, the two shadowscript spells will battle for dominance and create a Hyperhex storm. That storm will mutate into a merger spell between this world and Northern Fairyland and destroy them both."

"You don't know that for sure!"

"Oh, but I do; I heard enough from my gaolers and I've seen enough of my books coming to life to see where this is leading."

Mr Mystico turned to face me and Flumpkin, again.

"We haven't got much time," he said. "We've got to find Clutterbutt and then I've got to take my computer and the both of you to this printer's place I know near Hyde."

"What use'll that be?" asked Flumpkin.

"The first shadowscript is like a magical contract," said Mr Mystico. "It relies on me writing a final installation in the Flumpkin – sorry, yours and Clutterbutt's series and publishing it. It was always my intention to send the two of you back to Northern Fairyland and until that happens, the link between this world and yours will remain closed. If I'm right, Narkarla's shadowscript relies on me failing to publish. It also relies on her and her coven succeeding in their sacrifice. I think Flumpkin, you were the vessel they needed for their sacrifice so if you are sent back to Northern Fairyland my shadowscript spell will win and they won't succeed."

Flumpkin went a shade of green.

"If I succeed in printing off even a few books," Mr Mystico went on. "I can fulfil the first shadowscript contract and send you and Clutterbutt back home. Narkarla's contract will be broken and her spell will fail. If we're lucky we'll be able to save two worlds tonight."

"This printer you mentioned," said Mrs Creevely. "You said it was near Hyde. Isn't there a closer one?"

"It'll have to be Rylance's," said Mr Mystico. "They won't let me near anywhere else, and anyway, I know how to operate the equipment there."

"You'll need a wand, too," said Mrs Macbeth. "They took the fairy's wand and with all due respect, those two paintbrushes might be magical but they're not going to open a link between worlds – and another thing," she added. "What if you come across Narkarla and the rest of the coven? Those brushes'll be no match against a Triple Hex Sisterhood."

"We can take Clutterbutt's wand," said Flumpkin in an eager voice. "We need to pick him up anyway. Oh, I can't wait to go back home!"

Mrs Creevely stood up.

"It's decided then," she said, handing Mr Mystico a set of keys. "Mrs Macbeth and Splooshy, I want you to stay here and look after the elves. The rest of you; take my car; get that computer; get that wand and go to Rylance's but please be careful. I'm going to call up some reinforcements from here to see if we can assist in any way."

"Whose we?" I asked.

"The elf police, Guy," said Mr Mystico disprovingly. "Goodness me, when did you last read one of my Flumpkin and Clutterbutt books?"

"You'd better hurry up as well," said Mrs Macbeth pointing at the window.

I followed the direction of her finger, it was as though night had fallen.

"Since when on midsummer's eve does it go dark before five-o-clock?" I asked.

"Just as I thought," said Mr Mystico. "It's the start of the Hyperhex storm. The two shadowscript spells have started their war for dominance. If I'm right, any minute now, there'll be a massive power cut and all the lights will go out."

Two seconds later and right on cue, the room was plunged into darkness.

CHAPTER FOURTEEN – The Housekeeper's Reception

The drive back to my house was a sombre affair. None of us spoke a word. Whether it was the dark sky above, the occasional flash of lightning, the lack of any street lights or the fact that a massive beanstalk was growing in the middle of Warren Park I hadn't a clue.

Mr Mystico seemed to be concentrating on the road, Flumpkin looked lost in thought and I was thinking about Emma. All those times she'd been there for me: the time I ran away to Wales and they brought me back – only she had visited me in the private hospital; the time my mother had been reported missing in action – of all my friends only she came around and held my hand and only she had shared my relief when my mother turned up safe and well. Not once in all that time had I ever thanked her. True, I'd given her a gold crucifix last Christmas but that paled into insignificance next to the time she'd given me – and that was the thing – time. Love is not measured in baubles and jewels but time; the time you give someone, the time you spend with them.

Already once tonight, I'd come close to death and who knew what else would happen. If I was going to face death again tonight then there was one thing I had to do. It was to say thank you to Emma for all the things she'd done for me. She'd be at my house, waiting for me; just as she'd promised.

The car slowed to a halt.

"This is Regency Avenue where you live, Guy, isn't it?" said Mr Mystico. "My word, I must say, it is posh here."

I didn't reply. I just got out of the car, ran up the drive and opened the front door with my key. The house was in darkness.

"Emma!" I called. "Clutterbutt!"

The familiar gnawing sensation returned to my stomach. Something was wrong.

"Emma!" I called again.

"She's gone home, dearie," came a voice from the front room. I knew at once it belonged to Mrs Jenkins. I also remembered Mrs Macbeth's words, *That's why we've been watching you closely and the boy here, too.*

"What about Clutterbutt?" I called, testing the water.

"The fairy's gone, too!"

"Fairy? What do you mean, fairy?"

The hallway suddenly went cold and condensation formed on the mirror. There was a sound like air being released quickly from a balloon and before I knew it, Mrs Jenkins stood in front of me pointing a twisted wooden wand at my neck.

"I should have known not to entrust your custody to that fool Macbeth," she cackled. "As for your fairy and your girlfriend; even now as we speak they are being taken to my sister's hideaway." She waved her wand and added, "You, too, can now join them – fire whip!"

A sudden flash of orange and I felt as though a giant stretched elastic was pulling me back by the collar. I flew backwards, crashed into the mirror and fell in a heap beneath it. Fortunately it didn't break which was just as well; another seven years bad luck on top of this would have been too much.

My right cheek stung though and I could feel blood running down it.

"Ice blade," hissed Mrs Jenkins.

"Spell fade," came Mr Mystico's familiar voice, though he sounded a bit out of breath.

"Brush break!" retorted Mrs Jenkins. "And become a snake!" Mr Mystico howled.

"Brush attack, paint her black!" interjected Flumpkin.

"Brush shatter like crispy batter!"

Flumpkin squealed.

Enough was enough. I got off the floor and with my head down, seized Mrs Jenkins around the waist. Then calling on all my rugby training, I ran with all my might until we collided with the kitchen door. It burst open and we both tumbled to the floor. Something sharp stabbed me in the ribs and for a second, I struggled for breath. The room span and I retched.

"You fool!"

At last my breath came back. Slowly, the kitchen came back into focus. Mr Mystico was tying up Mrs Jenkins, pulling the cords 'til she winced in pain. What had happened? Had I missed something? Flumpkin stood looking over me, his forehead crinkled with concern.

"Thank goodness," he said. "I thought for a moment we'd lost you. I had to give you mouth to mouth resuscitation!"

"Pardon?"

I tried to get up, but my ribs screamed in agony and my body refused to comply.

"Here, let me help you," said Flumpkin. He looked at my ribs then gasped. "You're bleeding, Guy," he cried, "you're bleeding black blood."

"Well, what do you expect," cackled Mrs Jenkins. "He snapped my wand in two and he's got the splinters in him. I would say, at the very least, he's got ten minutes to live! Evil splinters always align with their evil sisters!"

"Mr Mystico," Flumpkin said in a strangled voice. "Give me your paint brush, quick!"

"I'm sorry," Mr Mystico retorted, tying the bonds so tight that Mrs Jenkins's howled in pain. "I had to stamp on its head! Remember?"

"But I need something; a wand, anything!"

"Can't you incantate?" asked Mr Mystico, pulling the bonds tighter.

"No, the spell's too powerful."

Big tears began rolling down Flumpkin's cheeks, causing his eye shadow to run. Black teardrops fell on my nose.

"Guy can't die, he's a good guy! He – he's almost like family to me. If only I had a wand!"

Wand! Family! There was something in that.

The room began spinning again and I vomited. My father was going to go ballistic when he saw the mess.

Wand! Family! Then I realised.

"Flumpkin," I said, struggling to form the words and holding back the urge to vomit again. "My grandfather's magic chest is in the attic. There's – there's wands in it – go and get them!"

"But, but you said yourself, he wasn't a proper magician."

I forced myself to grin in spite of the pain.

"Why do you have to be in denial all the time – trust me, my grandfather was probably the best magician in the country!"

The room began to go in and out of focus. Flumpkin ran sobbing upstairs and, a few minutes later, appeared carrying three long silver-tipped black wands. He waved one over me and started muttering something under his breath. Immediately the pain in my ribs subsided to a dull ache.

"These are brilliant!" he said.

"Told you," I said with a grin.

"He's still going to die, you know!" cackled Mrs Jenkins. "You're only delaying the inevitable!"

"Silence, witch!" snorted Mr Mystico, he tied a gag so tightly around her mouth, I thought her head was going to turn into an hour glass.

As for me, I was past caring. Life or death no longer mattered. The rest of the coven had Emma and Clutterbutt and now it was personal.

"Take her gag off!" I said.

"Pardon?"

An idea was slowly crystallising in my mind.

"Take it off!" I turned to Flumpkin and added, "Do you know any good spells that make people to tell the truth?"

Flumpkin shook his head.

Mrs Jenkins cackled.

The room began to spin and I felt a vein throbbing in my temple. The pain in my ribs returned and I felt my stomach beginning to rebel again.

"We're going to have to find out where they've taken Emma and Clutterbutt," I said, forcing my stomach into neutral.

"Do you think I'd really tell you?" hissed Mrs Jenkins.

Mr Mystico turned to face Flumpkin.

"Do you know any good pain spells?" he asked suddenly.

The colour drained from Flumpkin's face and I felt a lump in my throat. Mrs Jenkins cackled again.

"Torture me? You haven't got the guts, Melvyn Mystico!"

"We can't torture her!" I added.

"He's right," said Flumpkin. "You torture someone, you'd break a thousand laws of magic not to mention every single law of common decency. There's no way I could even bring myself to use a pain spell and torture her!"

"Listen!" said Mr Mystico. "Do you honestly think I like the idea? Think about it; unless we find Clutterbutt and get you and him back to your world, Narkarla is going to fulfil her contract at least in part. And what's going to happen then? If I'm right and I'm sure I am, both our worlds are going to be destroyed – sometimes, you have to put common decency aside to do what's right! Now for goodness sake, Flumpkin, do you know any pain or truth spells? We don't have time for a discussion on ethics - two worlds are at stake here!"

"Look, what makes you so sure?" I said in desperation.

"In my book, Narkarla takes three hostages. One's a girl called Victoria – that girl Victoria is actually based on a little girl I met once, a little girl who helped me out in a primary school some years back!"

"Emma?"

"Exactly!"

I gulped.

"And the other two?"

"Based on Di and Will of course – it was my way of saying thank you to the Flumpkin and Clutterbutt Appreciation Society! Now, Flumpkin, for goodness sake, if you know a spell, any spell, even a truth spell, tell it to me."

Flumpkin said nothing. Instead, he turned to Mrs Jenkins and waved his wand above her head. He muttered something inaudible and a kaleidoscope of unicorns, rainbows and golden sunflowers formed above her head. She shuddered then screamed and slumped forward. Tears welled up in Flumpkin's eyes as she let out another scream. I turned away and screwed my eyes shut. It was no good; her screams continued, louder and louder, pulling at the very fabric of my soul.

"I'll speak! I'll speak!" she screamed after what seemed like an eternity but in fact was only a few seconds.

"What on earth did you do to her?" asked Mr Mystico shocked by what we'd both witnessed.

"She was a little girl, too, once," said Flumpkin wiping his own tears away. "I used a return to innocence spell to try and rescue her from her witchiness but she fought it so hard it nearly killed her. She didn't want to return to innocence."

The witch sobbed.

"Narkarla has taken the fairy and the girl to a printing shop in Hyde. I know not what it's called. She intends to publish her shadowscript there tonight."

She spoke in short bursts, gasping for breath in between as though she'd run a marathon.

"And she believes blood sacrifices will make it more potent," Mrs Jenkins went on. "She's also sent some Sisters to take your friends in Concrete Close."

"But why take them?" I asked.

"Fool! Don't you see, they have consorted with wizards and have had a hand in the preparation of the shadowscript she is trying to defeat. Their sacrifice will make her shadowscript all the more potent."

"But I thought it was us she wanted to sacrifice."

"Idiot! You were meant as a sacrifice for something else more powerful, still. Your blood tomorrow at six minutes past seven in the morning would have been used to awaken the souls in the books – Narkarla would then have had a whole army at her disposal. An army such as like the world had never seen."

"The animalivrae," said Mr Mystico, his voice tinged with disgust. "Come on, we'd better get going. We've got to get to Concrete Close – with a bit of luck, the witches won't be there yet."

Mr Mystico's optimism; however, was short lived. The journey to Concrete Close was fraught with all sorts of hazards: twice we had to swerve to avoid rock goblins skittering about the road; on one occasion, a tall tower with a single window sprung up in the middle of the road and we had to take a detour; and to cap it all, we ran over the tail of some horned creature that looked suspiciously like a minotaur.

"It's the first phase of the Hyperhex storm," Mr Mystico explained as we turned at last into Concrete Close. "Some books are already starting to come alive in anticipation of the spell!" He then swore out loud.

I followed suit.

We were way too late.

Outside Di's house, with blue lights flashing were two police cars and an ambulance. Mr Mystico slammed the car to a halt and rushed into the house with Flumpkin. I went to dash in too, but a white-hot lancing pain shot up through my ribs and I had to lean on the car door for support.

"I don't believe it," said one stunned looking policeman standing nearby. "It looks like they've got a dead ogre in their living room."

"Guy, Guy, are you alright?"

A pair of arms grasped my shoulder. I knew from the wheezing breath it was Will. I looked up and saw him. Behind him, wide eyed and frightened stood Di's younger brother.

"Thank God!" I said. "Is Di safe?"

"Yes, yes, she's just coming out of the house with her dad; he's messed up a bit – fought off this massive creature, he did."

A trolley pushed past us. Hand firmly clasping her father's, Di barely noticed me. The big man was barely recognisable. His left eye was swollen and closed and his knuckles were bleeding. Gingerly, the medics lifted the stretcher into the back of the ambulance.

"Will," shouted Di. "Take care of Andy 'til mum gets back – take Guy in, too, he looks terrible. Guy, I phoned your house earlier – Emma's there safe with Clutterbutt."

Before I could tell her they'd been captured, the ambulance door closed and it sped off, siren wailing.

"What happened here?" I asked Will.

"We'd not long got back from looking for Mr Mystico, then it started going dark. There was a newsflash on telly and all of a sudden they were telling everyone to stay indoors that there's been some chemical spill or something. Anyway, next thing there was this almighty bang on Di's front door, then it crashed open and this ugly warty green monster came storming in with a really old lady. They tried to kidnap me and Di but woke Di's dad up instead – big mistake. He went berserk. The lady was obviously some sort of witch."

Will started to laugh.

"Di had a couple of canisters of pepper spray," he went on. "We squirted them in the witch's eyes and tied her up. The police have taken her away – what's been happening, Guy?"

Quick as I could, I told him.

"I'm coming with you," he said when I finished.

"Oh no you're not, young man," said a police constable suddenly appearing at our side. "There's been a pretty nasty animal attack here tonight and we need you to tell us in your own words exactly what happened." He then turned to me and added, "If you know what's good for you, lad, you'll get yourself home and lock all the doors, too – things are getting pretty crazy out here tonight."

He went to lead Will and Andy away but before he did, Will pressed something into my hand, winked and said, "Might come in handy!"

It was a can of pepper spray.

With my ribs still hurting, I put the canister into my pocket. What use it would be against a Triple Hex Sisterhood of witches I had no idea; but I was suffering so much, I didn't have the strength to throw it away. Fortunately, the pain in my ribs began to subside and to my enormous relief, I saw Mr Mystico running from the house with a laptop in his arms, closely followed by Flumpkin.

"We've run a quick check on the contents," panted Flumpkin. "Everything's there!"

Without another word we all bundled ourselves in Mrs Creevely's car, and with Mr Mystico behind the wheel, roared off.

"It'll take us a good twenty minutes to get to Rylance's," said Mr Mystico, putting the headlights onto full beam. "We're not going to have much time and I haven't got anything planned – any suggestions?"

"These wands are pretty powerful," Flumpkin replied. "We could put in a pretty hefty chaos grenade – watch out for that centaur!"

"Too risky," said Mr Mysico, swerving quickly to avoid the horse-like creature (it had stood stock still in the headlights like a frightened deer). "The last thing I want is for the machinery to start going crazy on me whilst I'm trying to print off a load of books!"

"We could try a nettle net."

"No, they'd magic up an antidote in no time – what about sleeping dust?"

Flumpkin shook his head.

"Witches tend to be fairly immune to that one, we'd probably end up putting ourselves to sleep instead and getting caught again."

"Extreme rigour?"

"We'd have to get really close and there's too many of them – they'd turn us into frogs before we could do half of them!"

Flumpkin and Mr Mystico continued discussing spells and discounting them one by one. My ribs still twinged and, every so often, would erupt into a cloud of white-hot pain. All my pride at having performed two really good spells earlier had by now disappeared and I realised just how much I really knew – which was very little. How easy it would have been, I thought, if we could have just done the job without having to do magic as well.

Outside of the car, things seemed to be getting crazier and crazier: A gang of council workmen armed with chainsaws were trying to corner a particularly vicious-looking oak tree that spat and snarled at them; a three-foot man with long pointy shoes and an old-fashioned spinning wheel over his shoulder was running away from two policemen; and further down the road, three brown bears dressed in lederhosen were scurrying out of a ram raided electrical goods shop carrying a fridge, a flat-screen TV and a laptop computer between them.

"I'm telling you," said Mr Mystico, his patience now starting to leave him. "Holy water frozen into ice shards and enchanted with a Level Seven witch attractant will do the job."

"It has to be proper holy water," shouted Flumpkin. "Triply distilled into a flask of diamond and decanted into a pure silver vial - where on earth in Manchester are you going to get that?"

If only we didn't need to do magic I thought. Small wonder the elves didn't like magic. It made life so complicated – oh, for a life without magic.

And then it hit me like a ton of bricks. The very first Flumpkin and Clutterbutt book I'd ever read: *"Oh come on, please," moaned Flumpkin, his blue eyes wet with tears. "How were we to know the anti-magic charm had been lifted for restoration…"*

That was it! An anti-magic charm cast upon the printer's! Without their magic, the witches would be just a bunch of relatively harmless ladies; and with a bit of luck, mostly old ones at that. I could create a diversion, Flumpkin could free the others and Mr Mystico could print off his book. We could then meet up outside the printer's, open up the portal and send the two fairies back to their world.

"Listen," I said.

Quickly I told the others my plan, pausing only the once whilst Mr Mystico reversed up a street to avoid two enormous pairs of legs, each dragging a massive tree trunk behind them.

"It's not a bad idea," said Flumpkin. "I've never heard of anyone putting the anti-magic charm on a whole building before but with these wands and between the three of us – I'm sure we can do it.

"We'll soon find out how effective it is, then" said Mr Mystico. "There's Rylance's up ahead in the distance."

CHAPTER FIFTEEN - The Battle at Rylance's

In the distance, Rylance's looked more like a gothic castle than a printing factory. Round turrets pierced the night sky, and the massive arched wooden gates set in the square wall resembled a massive drawbridge. High above in the inky black sky, a dark cloud with a shiny green lining hovered above, bathing the building in an iridescent green glow that made it stand out among all the other tall shadowy structures like a Halloween beacon.

We stopped about two hundred yards from the wooden gate.

"It looks almost like they're expecting us," whispered Flumpkin, getting out of the car and drawing his wand.

Clutching my painful, sticky ribs, I got out too and both Mr Mystico and I drew our wands, anticipating the spell we both knew surely must come in the next few minutes. Would it be strong enough, I wondered. Would we be able to stop the witches in time and save my friends from Narkarla's evil sacrifice?

"There's nothing to the spell really," said Flumpkin. "We need to hold the wand tips together for about thirty seconds and hum quietly in order to get them to work in harmony; and then we need to point them at the factory and say, "protect from magic, hex and curse, seal this shield inside the verse" – one other thing," he added. Mr Mystico, you point to the left, I'll point at that turret on the right, and Guy, I want you to point your wand above the big wooden gate. Are you ready? One – two – three…ummmmmmm…"

We did as Flumpkin said and then as one, pointed our wands and recanted the verse.

Nothing happened.

"Try again," said Flumpkin. "Only this time, when you're saying the verse, you must imagine your chest has opened out to reveal your heart and the magic is flowing out of it with each beat like a mountain spring. Once again; one – two – three…ummmmm…"

This time, the change was immediate. The green lining around the huge inky-black cloud disappeared and Rylance's was plunged into darkness.

"Okay, let's go for it," said Mr Mystico pulling his laptop out of the car and turning to run.

Another cloud of white-hot pain coursed through my ribs. How I managed to keep my legs going and keep up with the other two, I had no idea. It didn't matter though; somewhere inside that building, my friends were in danger.

"There's a smaller entrance to the right," said Mr Mystico, already starting to pant a little. "It's a tradesman's entrance and will take us into a corridor. I need to go right, to find the emergency generator and my workshop."

"You've got your own workshop?" said Flumpkin.

"Well, what do you expect? With my last book Splooshy the Squirrel, I only printed about two hundred copies – I don't know whether you've noticed, but my books aren't exactly selling like hot cakes at the moment!"

We reached the tradesmen's entrance but found it locked. Flumpkin tried his invisible key trick and cursed when it didn't work.

"At least we know the spell was successful," said Mr Mystico, pulling a key out of his pocket. "I was such a regular customer here, they gave me this to come and go as I pleased." He opened the door then turned to us and added, "If I'm right, Narkarla is going to be in the main print workshop. You need to go down the left corridor and keep going. She can't do anything yet because the power's still down. Give me half an

126

hour, that should be long enough to print off a dozen books then meet me back at the car – now good luck!"

Flumpkin and I watched Mr Mystico disappear then ran down the left corridor, trying to keep our footfalls as silent as possible. It was just as dark as the sealed off corridor back in my school. The blue emergency light from the battery-powered lanterns on the wall cast-off weird shadows that seemed to dance and mock us.

"Should be nearly there now," whispered Flumpkin. "Leave me to do the diversion. I'm going to lead them a merry dance, and as soon as the coast is clear, you go free your friends.

"What are you going to do?" I asked.

Flumpkin stopped and pulled a top hat and some silk scarves from his school bag.

"It wasn't just your grandfather's wands that I borrowed," he whispered with a grin.

We carried on and pretty soon reached a set of double doors. Each had a small window illuminated in a dull orange glow and beneath them was a sign telling people not to wear loose articles of clothing. Above the doors was another sign and it read:

MAIN PRINT WORKSHOP.

With our noses pressed to the window, we could see our job wasn't going to be an easy one. The inside of the print factory was like the inside of a massive airport terminal. Four or five figures in black robes and hoods stood around a long metallic bench that ended in what almost resembled a sperm whale's loo roll. On the other side of the bench was a raised metallic deck with railings.

Further back on the raised platform stood a tall-black-robed figure in the tallest pointiest witch's hat I had ever seen.

"There's Narkarla," whispered Flumpkin.

She clutched in her left hand a gnarled wooden sceptre that ended in a pearly white sphere the size of a large orange. Even in the shadow you couldn't but notice how the pallor of her smooth face shone in the eerie half-light like a full moon in a cloudless sky. And if it wasn't for her jet-black eyebrows, wisps of black hair and the fact she was talking into a megaphone, I'd have sworn she was a ghost.

"Can you see Emma and Clutterbutt?" I whispered, rubbing my still painful ribs.

Flumpkin pointed to the far side of the factory. At first, all I could see in the dim light was a wall of palettes full of paperbacks; each palette shrink-wrapped in cellophane and stacked one on top of the other as high as the ceiling. Just in front of these and to the left was a fork lift truck. Emma and Clutterbutt were standing tied back to back to a tall metal pillar right behind the vehicle's half-raised forks.

"This is my plan," whispered Flumpkin. "We wait ten minutes to give Mr Mystico time to get his machinery running then I go in there and cause the diversion. With a bit of luck, they've all chase after me then as soon as the coast is clear, you go in and free Emma and Clutterbutt."

Suddenly, there were several flickers and the corridor and the factory beyond the doors were flooded in light. The machinery on the shop floor hummed into life, and the witches started flicking switches so that the giant loo roll of paper began turning like a spit-roasted chicken.

"At last, it begins!"

With a triumphant grin, Narkarla reached inside her robes and produced a long-twisted dagger. The blade shone with a midnight blue and seemed to hum so that its echo resonated on the machinery, cheering it on, willing it to work quicker. Even at the distance, the malevolence reflected in Narkarla's eyes was unmistakable. Slowly, she surveyed the scene in front of her then said in a measured, high pitched voice, "I cannot delay the sacrifice much longer. Vilesteel here craves his blood and must be sated."

"Change of plan, wish me luck," whispered Flumpkin pulling on my grandfather's black top hat. Before I could say anything else, he pushed open the doors, strode onto the factory floor and shouted, "Good evening, good evening, my name is Mr Wando the Magician. Somebody gave me a phone call saying there was a magical theme party here tonight…"

"Seize him!" screeched Narkarla from her deck.

Every witch made a grab for Flumpkin and he took off like a jet propelled squirrel. I couldn't believe my eyes at how quickly he moved: ducking under machinery, flicking the switches off and causing two witches to run smack bang into one another; upsetting a can of oil and causing another witch to slip on it so forcefully she skidded head first into the front wheel of the fork lift truck; and finally climbing up and down a stack of empty palettes like a mountain goat and dashing through a far exit.

"After him, you fools," screeched Narkarla. "Use your magic if you must! We cannot afford to have our location leaked to the elves, not now we're so near!"

The other witches maintained their pursuit and soon only Narkarla was left inside the large factory room along with Clutterbutt and Emma. Slowly, the witch began her descent down the steps from the deck to the workfloor, swishing her dark dagger up and down and side to side as she did so; so that it hummed even louder.

Gritting my teeth, I reached into my pocket and pulled out the can of mace. The pain in my ribs started to ache with a new level of intensity and I wanted to scream out but it wouldn't have been any use. Every single policeman and fireman in Manchester was probably occupied outside with the magical fallout of the recent storm and not one of them would have heard me. Every sense in my body screamed at me to run away; that cowards lived on to fight another day. But if what Mr Mystico had said was true, then there wouldn't be another day after this. So with another painful deep breath, I pushed open the doors and strode onto the factory floor.

"You!"

"Guy!"

Emma's scream of warning echoed against the stacks of books on palettes. Narkarla glared at me with wide eyes as though I had walked into a bank and caught her with her fingers in the till.

"Give it up, Narkarla, you know what I am," I shouted, hoping my voice wouldn't betray the fear I felt inside. And then another idea struck me. "Give it up, Narkarla, we've told the police what's going on and they'll be here any minute."

"Then it's your corpse they'll discover and take home to your mother," cackled the witch, pointing her crystal staff at me.

Nothing happened, and she held up the end of the staff in front of her face, examining the white sphere with her eyes and mouth wide open. I was momentarily reminded of the bad guys in the cartoons and half expected it to blow up on her – it didn't unfortunately.

"Well whaddya know," she hissed. "Protected from magic but aren't you forgetting something, silly boy?"

She vaulted over the rail, then spread her arms and legs in mid air as though she were about to take off like a huge vampire bat. Big mistake! She plummeted to the concrete floor below and hit the ground with a resounding splat. Slowly and looking totally bewildered, she picked herself up; her staff now broken in two by her side.

I tried another bluff.

"Your magic is powerless in my presence, Narkarla, give yourself up while you still can." I shouted.

A briefest shadow of doubt crossed her face and my heart started beating faster. Maybe, just maybe, my ruse was going to work.

It didn't. Another cloudburst of agony erupted. This time, it wasn't just confined to my ribs, it seemed to course through my whole body; starting at the tip of my toes and erupting out of my ears like a cascade from a fractured dam. It hurt so much I wanted to be sick and before I knew it, my legs had turned to jelly. An instant later, they gave way beneath me and gravity propelled me to the cold concrete embrace below. Something else clattered, and I knew immediately I'd lost my can of mace.

In the space of a heartbeat, Narkarla was standing above me, her dark hissing twisted dagger held at an angle ready to strike.

"I see black blood on your shirt," she hissed. "Evil splinters always align with their evil sisters." She cackled a high pitch cackle then added, "Perhaps your powers are not as sharp as you claim. Nevertheless, Vilesteel here will enjoy drinking what's left of your life and your soul…"

She slashed and I rolled with every last ounce of strength I could muster. As I did so, something hard and round dug into my ribs. For an instant, I thought the dagger had found its mark then I realised what it was.

In desperation, I plunged my hand down and my fingers made contact with the welcoming cold steel of the mace can. Without a second thought, I held it up and pressed the release button.

Nothing happened. Damn, I hadn't pulled out the pin.

There was another humming swish as Vilesteel tried to find my throat. I rolled again and took aim. This time I didn't forget the pin.

"Eeeargh!"

Narkarla's scream caused an ice chill to descend on the entire factory, and for an instant, I wondered if the anti-magic charm had died. Like a wounded velociraptor, she vigourously clawed at her eyes and, in doing so, dropped her weapon. The black blade fell to the floor with a clatter. In an instant, I picked it up, then half running, half crawling, I moved over to the pillar where Emma and Clutterbutt were tied.

"Wrists first," hissed Emma.

"Feet first," squeaked Clutterbutt. "I can run on those."

The dagger tried to rebel in my hands as I cut Emma's and Clutterbutt's bonds. Almost like two powerful magnets being placed together at the same poles. How I managed to avoid hurting either of them, I didn't know because the blade cut like a razor and made short work of the rope.

"Which way out?" said Clutterbutt shaking the remains of his bonds from his wrists.

"This way!" I gasped, pointing to the door through which I'd come.

"Guy, you're hurt," said Emma suddenly, her voice half-choking.

"I'll be fine – let's go!"

With Narkarla's screams echoing in our ears we made our way quickly back to the corridor. It took me a few seconds to realise the other two were supporting me and tried to break free in embarrassment, only to go stumbling to the ground again.

"No time for heroics," said Clutterbutt, helping me up. "Where does this corridor lead?"

"To Mr Mystico," I said. "It's a long story!"

As we went along, I gasped out as much as I could about the shadowscripts and how important it was for Mr Mystico to get his copies printed off.

"We'd better get back to him," said Clutterbutt. He might need a hand carrying the copies back to the car.

It didn't take us long to find where he'd gone. We followed the sound of humming machinery to a door. It stood slightly ajar with a light on behind. Above a sign read: SMALL SCALE PRINT WORKSHOP.

"It must be here," I said.

We pushed the door open and were immediately met by a bang and a flash. To me, it was as though someone had tied a tight elastic bungee cord to my waist, the way I flew backwards. Gasping with a new realisation, I reached into my pocket for my wand. Someone had used magic on us – that I knew. But how? We'd put an anti-magic charm on the building. A dark silhouette appeared in the doorway to the workshop. I pointed the wand and shouted, "Back!"

"I think you'll find your powers somewhat depleted, dearie, after that wound I gave you! Evil splinters always align with their evil sisters."

"Mrs Jenkins?"

"Exactly. You should have tied me up a bit tighter!"

Several more witches appeared at her side and I was picked up forcibly and thrown into the room next to Emma and Clutterbutt. Mr Mystico lay on the ground beside us, motionless.

"As you can see," Mrs Jenkins went on. "On my way here, I gathered a few reinforcements. I must say, I'm surprised you've lived so long. Even with magical healing, evil splinters from a dark wand usually kill a lot quicker. You must have a very powerful magic in you."

"Not much use though, was it?" I snarled.

"Foolish boy! Don't you know when you suffer a magical wound your own magic turns inwards to combat it, rendering you powerless," snapped one of the witches.

The others cackled as though sharing some obnoxious joke together. Behind them, the printing press machinery hummed away. I hoped beyond hope Mr Mystico had got his novel into the machinery to print.

"Now," said Mrs Jenkins, pushing her face close up to mine so I could smell her rancid breath. "Tell me where that other fairy friend of yours is. I want to give my friends here a lesson in torture and since he's such an expert in the field, I'm sure he'll make an excellent subject."

"I don't know," I replied.

"What's that?" snapped Mrs Jenkins suddenly holding Narkarla's black blade to my throat. "I can't hear you with the noise in this place."

More white-hot pain coursed through my veins, and I found myself wondering if it was magic being used against me or the ongoing result of the magical splinters.

"I don't know!" I gasped.

"Tell me!"

More pain. In the corner of my eye, I noticed Mr Mystico getting up on his forearms. It then occurred to me if I could create a diversion he might be able to escape with the others.

"Leave him, he's mine!"

The voice was cold and sibilant like an eloquent python. Narkarla strode into the room, black cloak swishing behind her. She glared at me through bloodshot eyes, which then fell on the object Mrs Jenkins was holding.

"That's my dagger, Vilesteel, give it me back," she demanded.

Mrs Jenkins jumped up, clutching the dagger to her chest like a baby.

"It's mine, now! I won it in a fair fight against this wizard!"

"He didn't win it from me fairly though so it's not his to yield!" retorted Narkala.

The two witches stared at each other. Face like thunder, eyes glowing with malice. Through the pain in my ribs an idea hit me like a ton of bricks.

"I won it fairly from you, it was a fair fight," I shouted.

"No, he didn't!"

"Oh yes, I did!"

"He didn't," shrieked Narkarla.

"Oh yes, he did," laughed Clutterbutt getting in on the act.

"It's mine, I tell you!" shrieked Mrs Jenkins.

"Oh no, it isn't," said Emma.

"Oh yes, it is," laughed Clutterbutt.

A split second later, the two witches started fighting, literally going at each other like alley cats, screaming, biting, slapping, slashing and tearing. The other witches desperately tried to pull them apart.

"Go," I said to Mr Mystico. "Take Emma and Clutterbutt and get them as far away from here as possible."

He went to push them towards the door but Emma pulled away.

"I'm not going without you, Guy," she said, tears streaming down her face.

The pleading look in her green eyes was too much. All I wanted was to sleep for a month and I could feel the black blood oozing cold on my stomach.

"It's alright, I'll catch you up," I lied, holding tight the sticky black hole in my shirt. "I've just got one last trick to hold them up!"

"Be careful, Guy!" hissed Clutterbutt.

"Come on," hissed Mr Mystico. "Guy's got it under control!"

Quickly, they exited the room though Emma had to be forcibly pushed. Ten seconds later, the sound of machinery went dead.

"Look!" said one of the witches with a gasp.

I followed the direction of her long finger. There on a motionless conveyer belt with their spines facing us were a dozen paperbacks. Each one bore the title: "Flumpkin and Clutterbutt go Home".

"Enough," snapped Narkarla snatching the dagger. She drew her wand and flicked it in the direction of the books which subsequently exploded in clouds of burning sparks. "Sisters," she commanded. "Take this prisoner back to the print room.

There is still time for us to finish our work here tonight, but we must hurry!"

I was yanked forcibly to my feet and hurriedly dragged down the corridor back to the main factory.

"Ignore the others," commanded Narkala. "We can get them later. This one will suffice for now!"

The pain in my ribs was so unbearable I didn't care whether I lived or died as the witches pushed me in a reclining position to some flat piece of machinery. I half-struggled against two pairs of hands in a hopeless attempt to break free; however, a swift right hook from Mrs Jenkins sent me back into the reclining position. I looked on as Narkarla held her dark blade aloft. I should have been afraid but all I could think of was Emma and the others. I closed my eyes and willed them to escape. Still willing and willing and willing them to get as far away as possible from Rylance's I heard Narkala say:

"Spirits of darkness, hear my plea.

"Give thy power and strength to me.

"The blood of this wizard will forever serve,

"To prove to thee of my true worth…"

There was a blinding flash and suddenly I was aware of what looked like a hundred steel robots storming into the factory. Narkarla's eyes widened in fear and she immediately went to plunge her dagger into my heart, but it inexplicably flew from her grasp. A split second later and a net made from what looked like spider's web engulfed her and she fell to the floor, arms and legs flailing like a fish doing a fast-foot fandango… I'd succeeded. Everyone was safe. The room span and the pain took on a new intensity, I felt tired like that undefined moment between wakefulness and falling asleep… a helpless, inexorable drifting… so this was what the end of life looked like… on the bright side, at least I wouldn't have to go back to Tremerwick Towers!

CHAPTER SIXTEEN – The Strangest of Places

A song sung by what sounded like a Welsh male voice choir filled my mind. I opened my eyes and the walls of a room came into focus. They were polished gold festooned with rubies, emeralds and huge rainbow-coloured opals. Heavy, shiny silk cream-coloured curtains laced with gold thread hung over huge windows like tapestries in a medieval castle and although they were drawn, the sun still somehow managed to shine through causing the gold and jewels on the walls to glitter like a thousand stars singing on a clear summer night at sea.

So this is what heaven looked like.

Female voices joined with the male voices in harmony and I was reminded of some of the songs I'd heard as a toddler. My stomach clenched and I thought of my mother and father and my sister and brother. We'd not always seen eye-to-eye but I wished I'd spoken to them one last time. Wished I'd apologised to my father for being such a horrible son all those times I ran away from Tremerwicks. I realised now I must have put both my parents through the worst kind of hell and how I wished I could have said goodbye one last time. What would they say now, I wondered? Would they have found my battered and bloodied body in the aftermath of the Hyperhex storm? Would they have had a chance to see me and say goodbye, too? My eyes welled up and I could see my mother's tears, almost feel them falling onto my own lifeless body like raindrops on autumn leaves fallen in some long-forgotten forest. I could see Emma crying, as well, her arms round my mother and father comforting them, secretly chiding me for lying to her with my final words.

"I'm sorry," I whispered, feeling hot tears streaming down my cheeks.

"No need to be sorry, Guy."

I looked around.

There stood an elderly man whose bright blue eyes matched the blue of the robes he wore. His white beard glistened in the silk-filtered sunlight illuminating a scar on his left cheek and long grey hair fell about his shoulders like an aging heavy rock star. So this was heaven after all.

"Grandfather?" I said. "You're dead, aren't you?"

My grandfather laughed.

"No, I am most evidently alive," he replied. "Otherwise I wouldn't be standing beside you in this very delightful place."

"I'm – er – alive then?" I enquired.

My grandfather laughed again.

"Most evidently so, otherwise I am sure you wouldn't be attempting to talk with me. I must confess we were all worried at one point, though."

The room started to spin and I felt a peculiar need to vomit again.

"Where am I?" I asked.

"You are in the Tower of Healing, at good Queen Mabiley's Court in Northern Fairyland," my grandfather replied. "You are very lucky to be alive. Had the knight protectors not gotten to you sooner, I fear the evil splinters would have done their work. As it is, you will likely be here for at least another month."

"Did we beat the witches, then?" I asked. "Did Mr Mystico's shadowscript beat Narkarla's and open up the gateway?"

To my surprise, my grandfather shook his head.

"Alas, no," he replied. "You probably saw yourself the destruction of his first print job which incidentally, should any have survived will most likely be worth a handsome sum by now. The story of your battle at Rylance's will undoubtedly keep the scribes and poets here busy for decades to come."

"But I don't understand…" I began.

"You see," my grandfather continued. "To all intents and purposes, Narkarla's shadowscript was a lot stronger than Mr Mystico's which is only to be expected from such a powerful witch. But if you are wondering, if she was defeated, then yes, she is now back in a proper environment for witches at one of the reservations in Southern Fairyland."

"How was she beaten then?" I asked.

"She was beaten by a very powerful magician probably one of the most powerful who has ever lived."

"You?" I ventured.

My grandfather laughed and shook his head.

"It was you, Guy," he replied. "It was your magic and your magic alone that overcame the two shadowscripts."

"But how?" I asked. "The witches said the evil splinters caused my magic to turn in on myself and rendered it unusable. I couldn't stop them and if it hadn't been for the knight protectors capturing Narkarla, she would have succeeded."

My grandfather put his hand on my shoulder and my nausea lifted.

"On the contrary, Guy," he said with a genial smile. "On the night, it was you who performed the strongest spell of all, and you who allowed the gateway to open for the knight protectors to go in. Perhaps you could tell me what it was you think you did?"

I shook my head.

"Not even hazard a guess?"

I shook my head again.

"It was your pure heroism, Guy," he said. "Your willingness to sacrifice yourself for your friends, even your willingness to lie to those you loved most to keep them from harm. These in themselves are acts of the truest love performed with the purest of intentions and in the truest love you will always find the strongest magic. That much has always been obvious to those of us who study Higher Magyck and has been so since time began. When faced with such a potent force, both shadowscripts didn't have a chance; they were completely eclipsed and fell apart and the gateway opened – so it was your one true act that broke the four-year spell."

My index finger twinged and I looked at the scar from the craft knife.

"Was it us who blocked the gateway in the first place?" I asked. "That time when we wrote the first story with Mr Mystico?"

My grandfather shook his head.

"No, that was Narkala. Just after Flumpkin and Clutterbutt arrived in your world on suspension she sealed the gateway with very dark magic. She was on an exchange visit to your world but it had always been her ambition to set up a new sisterhood. Ironically, I was the exchange student and I was stuck here in Northern Fairyland as a result."

"Am I stuck here, too?" I asked alarmed at the prospect of maybe never seeing my friends again. Truth be told, I'd rather go to Tremerwick Towers, at least then I'd see my friends in the holidays.

"No, you will be free to come and go. The gateway is now open and secure and trade between the two worlds has resumed. Officially, you are here to recuperate for a month and then you will return. Mrs Creevely has kindly fixed it so people think you have been suspended and gone back to Tremerwick Towers after the damage to your father's Mercedes but rest assured you will be back at Eleven Hills next September with your friends where you belong. Now talking of friends, there are two special friends who I think want to say hello and thank you."

A huge door opened and Cluttebutt and Frumkin charged in, jumped on the bed and each gave me the biggest hug a fairy could possibly give a guy.

"Steady on, boys," said my grandfather. "He's still recuperating."

"We made it, Guy," laughed Clutterbutt.

"We're both knight protectors, now," grinned Flumpkin. "And it's all thanks to you."

"Oh, you brave boys did your part, too," laughed my grandfather. "Mrs Jenkins is still in intensive therapy after that flatulence charm you put on her broom, Clutterbutt and as for you, Mr Flumpkin: Narkarla is still trying to magic off those sideburns you put on her. Indeed, I wouldn't be surprised if she's thinking of auditioning for one of those 1970s disco revival groups even as we speak."

Both fairies laughed, their eyes glinting full of mischief.

"Well," said my grandfather. "I must be getting along. I have a lecture to give on Higher Magyck at the Queen Mabiley University of Magyck and Illusion. I'll see you again, tomorrow, Guy."

"Have a mint imperial before you go, Magi-Professor Foulkstone," said Clutterbutt offering my grandfather an open paper bag.

"Don't mind if I do," he replied taking one of the white balls and putting it towards his mouth. He paused for a second and added, "this isn't one of your Magi-Grow Elephant Trunk tricks, is it by any chance? Only it would be most embarrassing standing in front of three hundred students trumpeting away even if it would ensure they all stayed awake!"

Both fairies shook their heads.

"And it isn't some other cheeky prank by any chance?"

"Fairies honour," they both replied raising their left hands. I couldn't help but notice their right hands behind their backs with their fingers crossed.

My grandfather ate the sweet and left the room with a swish of his long white hair. He closed the door behind him. Two seconds later there was the loudest belch I'd ever heard and the door knob rattled.

"You pair of rascals!" came his voice from down the corridor.

"Your grandfather is so cool," said Clutterbutt.

"I can't believe you're a really powerful wizard, too, Guy," said Flumpkin. "Does that mean you'll be staying here with us?"

I shook my head and told them everything my grandfather had told me. it would be at least a month before I could see my friends again.

"You really miss them, don't you," said Clutterbutt.

"Who," I replied.

"Emma, Will, Di, Mr Mystico..."

I nodded my head wishing more than anything else we could be in the cinema or in Di's shed holding another meeting of the Flumpkin and Clutterbutt Appreciation Society. The two fairies whispered to one another for a few seconds then turned around; huge beaming grins on their faces.

"Not to worry," said Flumpkin. "We've got a plan."

"Yes," said Clutterbutt. "Your grandfather's comment on a 1970s disco revival group gave us an idea. We're going to smuggle them into Northern Fairyland and the palace here under the guise of a cultural visit. Now, we're going to need a lumberjack outfit, a Canadian Mountie outfit, a fireman's outfit..."

I couldn't help but laugh aloud as they continued hatching their plan. Deep down. Something told me the new adventures of the Flumpkin and Clutterbutt Appreciation Society were only just beginning.

THE END

TABLE OF CONTENTS